Tales from the Enchanted World

For my parents

Tales from the Enchanted World

AMABEL WILLIAMS-ELLIS

Illustrated by
MOIRA KEMP

Little, Brown and Company
BOSTON   TORONTO

First U.S. Edition

First published in Great Britain in 1987 by Hodder and Stoughton Ltd

The Great White Cat, Childe Rowland, The Well of the World's End and
The Bear in the Coach first published 1950 in *PRINCESSES AND TROLLS*

*Cap o' Rushes, The King, the Saint and the Goose, Johnny-Cake, Mr. Miacca,
The Laidly Worm of Spindlestone Heugh, White-Faced Siminy, Tamlane,
The Fifty Red Night-Caps* and *Tom-Tit-Tot* first published 1960 in
FAIRY TALES OF THE BRITISH ISLES

Baba Yaga and *Anansi and Mrs. Dove* first published 1963 in
ROUND THE WORLD FAIRY TALES

The Country of the Mice and *The Magic Bird* first published 1966 in
OLD WORLD AND NEW WORLD FAIRY TALES

My Berries and *The Great Greedy Beast* first published 1977 in
THE RAINGOD'S DAUGHTER

The Master Thief, The Three Sisters and *The Waterfall* first published
in this compilation

Library of Congress Catalog Card No. 87-82561

ISBN 0-316-94133-6

Printed in Italy

Contents

Foreword

*A*MABEL WILLIAMS-ELLIS *was born into a literary family. Her father was St. Loe Strachey, Editor of* The Spectator *for many years. She wrote many books for adults and children. She was fascinated by scientific developments until she died in 1984 at the age of eighty-six. She was married to the well-known architect Sir Clough Williams-Ellis.*

Lady Williams-Ellis will be best remembered for her story-telling. She traveled extensively and collected folk tales and legends from all the places she visited. She paid particular attention to local versions of stories and took a lot of trouble to find out as much as she could about sources and the history of the stories she collected.

Several collections were published, including Round the World Fairy Tales, Old World and New World Fairy Tales, *and* Fairy Tales from the British Isles. *One of her aims was to help children to increase their understanding of countries other than their own.*

The stories in this collection were chosen during the last year of Amabel's life. She included some old favorites as well as some less well-known but traditional tales. She aimed to give the greatest pleasure to the greatest possible number of her readers.

Cap o' Rushes

THERE WAS ONCE a very rich gentleman, and he had three daughters.

One day he thought he would like to see how fond they each were of him. So he says to the first:

"How much do you love me, my dear?"

"Why," says she, "I love you as I love my life."

"That's good," says he. So he says to the second, "How much do you love me, my daughter?"

"Why," says she, "I love you better than all the world."

"That's good," says he. So he says to the third, "How much do *you* love me, my dear?"

Now the youngest daughter didn't like this sort of question, and she didn't believe that her sisters really loved their father as much as she did. She tried to laugh it off, so she said:

"I love you as much as fresh meat needs salt."

"That means you don't love me at all, you ungrateful thing!" says he, working himself to a passion. "In my house you shall stay no more!"

The end of it was that nothing she could say would persuade him of the truth, which was that she did love him the best, and he shut his door on her so that all she had got to go out into the wide world with were three dresses.

However, there was nothing for it, away she had to go. On and on she went, till she came to a watery, squelchy bog. And there she gathered

a lot of rushes, and she plaited them up till she made a kind of a cloak with a hood to it and, when she put it on, the cloak covered her from head to foot. After that she went up on to higher ground and hid her three fine dresses under the dry roots of a tree. Then on she went again till at last she came to a great house.

"Do you want a maid?" says she.

"No, we don't," says they.

"I haven't got anywhere to go," says she, "and I'd ask no wages, and do any sort of work."

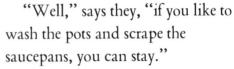

"Well," says they, "if you like to wash the pots and scrape the saucepans, you can stay."

So she stayed, and she washed the pots and scraped the saucepans, and did all the dirty work. And because she didn't tell them any name, they called her Cap o' Rushes.

One day there was to be a great dance a little way off, and the servants where she worked were allowed to go and look at the grand people. But Cap o' Rushes said she was too tired to go, so she stayed at home.

But when all the others were gone, she offed with her cap o' rushes and she washed herself in the clear water of the brook, and she went back to the fen and put on a silver dress and went to the ball. And of all the fine folk who were dancing there, there was none so fair or so finely dressed as she.

Who should be at the ball, but her master's son. And what should he do but fall in love with her the moment he set eyes on her. He wouldn't dance with anyone else.

But before the dance was done, Cap o' Rushes slipped off and away she went home. When the other maids got back she was pretending to be asleep with her cap o' rushes on.

Next morning, they said to her:

"You did miss a night, Cap o' Rushes!"

"What was that?" says she.

"Why, the beautifullest lady you ever did see, dressed right gay and gallant. The young master, he never took his eyes off her."

"Well, I should like to have seen her," says Cap o' Rushes.

"There's to be another dance this evening, and perhaps she'll be there."

But come the evening, Cap o' Rushes again said she was too tired to go with them. However, when they were gone, she offed with her cap o' rushes, washed herself in the brook, went back to the fen, and this time the dress she put on was one made all of gold.

The master's son had been reckoning on seeing her, and again he danced with no one else, and never took his eyes off her.

But before the dance was over, she slipped off.

Home she went once more, and, when the maids came back, she pretended to be asleep with her cap o' rushes on.

Next day they said to her again:

"Well, Cap o' Rushes, you should have been there to see the lady. There she was again, right gay and gallant. As for the young master, he never took his eyes off her."

"Deary me," says she. "I should like to have seen her!"

"Well," says they, "there's a dance again this evening, and you must go with us, for she's sure to be there."

Well, come the evening, Cap o' Rushes said for the third time that she was too tired to go, and do what the other servants would to persuade her, she said she would stay at home. But when they were all gone, for the third time she offed with her cap o' rushes, and bathed herself in the brook, went back to the tree, and this time put on a dress that was made of the feathers that had fallen from all the birds that fly in the air. And then, once more, away she went to the dance.

The master's son was overjoyed when he saw her. He danced with none other but her, and never took his eyes off her. But she wouldn't tell him her name, nor where she came from, but at last he gave her a ring, and told her if he didn't see her again he should die.

The dance wasn't over when she slipped away just as before. Home she went, and, for the third time, when the maids came back she was pretending to be asleep with her cap o' rushes on.

Next day they said to her:

"There, Cap o' Rushes! You didn't come last night, and now you won't see the lady, for there's to be no more dances."

"Well, I should rarely like to have seen her," says she.

The master's son tried every way to find out where the lady was gone, but go where he might, and ask whom he might, he never heard a thing about her. The end of it was he got paler and paler, and at last he had to keep to his bed he was so ill and all for the love of her.

"Make some gruel for the young master," they said to the cook. "He's very sick and near dying for love of the lady."

The cook had only just set about making the gruel when Cap o' Rushes came in.

"What are you doing?" asks she.

"I'm going to make some gruel for the young master," says the cook, "for it seems that he's near dying for love of the lady."

"Let me make it," says Cap o' Rushes.

Well the cook wouldn't at first, but at last she agreed; and so it was Cap o' Rushes that made the gruel. When she had made it, she slipped the ring into it on the sly, before the cook took it upstairs.

The young man drank it, and then he saw the ring at the bottom.

"Send for the cook," says he. So up she comes again.

"Who made this gruel?" says he.

"I did," said the cook, for she was frightened, you see, but he just looked at her.

"No, you didn't," says he. "Say who did, and you shan't be harmed."

"Well, then, 'twas Cap o' Rushes," says she.

"Send Cap o' Rushes here," says he. So Cap o' Rushes came up.

"Did you make the gruel?" says he.

"Yes, I did," says she.

"Where did you get this ring?" says he.

"From him that gave it me," says she.

"Who are you, then?" says the young man.

"I'll show you," says she. And she offed with her cap o' rushes, and there she was in her beautiful clothes, and her lovely long hair hung to her waist.

The master's son he got well very soon, and they were to be married in a little time. It was to be a very grand wedding, and everyone was asked from far and near. Cap o' Rushes' father was one of those that was asked. But nobody knew that he was the bride's father, for still she wouldn't tell anybody who she was.

But before the wedding she went to the kitchen.

"I want you to dress every dish of meat without putting a mite o' salt on it," says she.

"That'll be rare and nasty," says the cook.

"Never you mind for that," says she.

Well, the wedding day came, and they were married. And after they were married, all the grand company sat down to the wedding feast.

But when they began on the meat, it was so tasteless they couldn't eat it. Cap o' Rushes' father, he tried first one dish and then another, and then, what did he do but burst out crying.

"What's the matter?" said the master's son to him.

"Oh," says he, "I had a daughter, and I asked her how much she loved me! And she said, "As much as fresh meat needs salt." And I turned her away from my door, for I thought she meant she didn't love me. But now, I see that she meant she loved me best of all. And she may be dead now for aught I know."

"No, father, here she is!" says Cap o' Rushes.

And with that she started up from her place and she ran to him and put her arms round his neck.

And so they all lived happily ever after.

This tale is found in many countries. This version comes from Suffolk, England.

The Great White Cat

ONCE UPON A TIME, far away in the north of Norway, there was a hunter and he caught a big white bear, alive, in a trap. It was such a fine young bear that he hadn't the heart to kill it, so he thought he would take it to the King of Denmark for a present. So he tamed it, and a very good bear it was.

Now, as bear and man plodded along on their long, long journey to the court of the King of Denmark, they came, just on Christmas Eve, to the Dovrafell. Now the Dovrafell is a bad sort of a place at any time of the year. It's a wild moor, all bog and heather and rock, with hardly a tree for shelter, and it's worst of all in the dark of winter, with the wind roaring and a sky full of snow. However, they hadn't gone far when the hunter thought he saw a light. As he got nearer he saw it must be a candle in a cottage window. Very glad he was to see it, in a wild place like that with the snow coming on.

The hunter knocked at the door and greeted the man of the house politely, and asked if he could get houseroom there for his bear and himself.

"You might come and welcome," said the man, whose name was Halvor. "But deary me! We can't give anyone houseroom, not just now!"

"But it's perishing cold out here in the Dovrafell," said the hunter.

"So it is," said Halvor, "and I'm sorry for you, but we have a bad time in this house at this time of the year. Every Christmas, for years now, such a pack of Trolls come down upon us that we are always forced to flit out of the house ourselves! Deary me! These seven years we haven't had so much as a house over our own heads – not at Christmas – and often not a morsel of food. It's very hard on the poor children, so it is!"

"Oh," said the hunter, "if that's all, you can very well let in me and my bear. We're not afraid of Trolls. My bear's a quiet fellow. He can lie under the stove yonder, and I can sleep in that little side-room you have by the kitchen."

Well, at first, Halvor said it would never do, but it was growing so cold outside, and the hunter begged so hard, that at last he and his bear were allowed to stay. So in they came. The bear lay down, and the hunter sat by the stove while the woman of the house began to get ready their Christmas dinner with the three children helping her. The hunter thought it was a queer sight to watch them getting the good things ready, for they had never a smile on their faces though they had managed to get together quite a nice feast, so that the hunter's mouth watered. But neither the good woman nor the children nor Halvor were very cheerful about it all, for, you see, they feared that it would only be the Trolls that would get it after all.

Next day was Christmas Day and, sure enough, no sooner had they all sat down to their Christmas dinner than down came

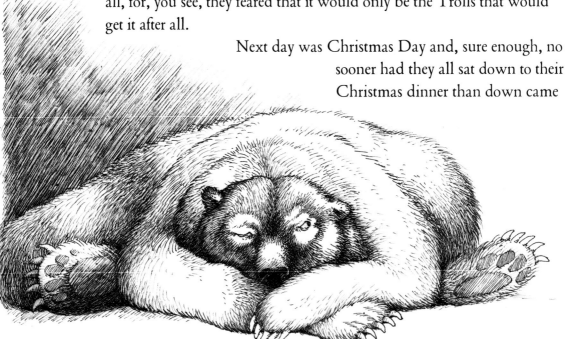

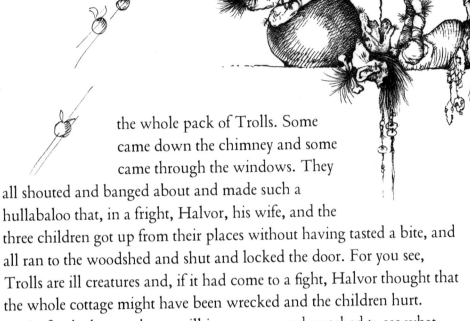

the whole pack of Trolls. Some
came down the chimney and some
came through the windows. They
all shouted and banged about and made such a
hullabaloo that, in a fright, Halvor, his wife, and the
three children got up from their places without having tasted a bite, and
all ran to the woodshed and shut and locked the door. For you see,
Trolls are ill creatures and, if it had come to a fight, Halvor thought that
the whole cottage might have been wrecked and the children hurt.

As for the hunter, he sat still in a corner, and watched to see what
would happen. Some of the trolls were big and some were little, and all
were black and hairy. Some had long tails, and some had no tails at all,
and some had noses as long as pokers. They all went on shouting and
they put their feet and their tails on the table, threw the food about, and
ate and drank, and messed and
tasted everything. The little,
screaming Trolls were the worst.
They pulled each other's tails,
fought over the food and even
climbed up the curtains and began
throwing such things as jars of jam

and pickles, *smash*, off the kitchen shelves.

At last, one of these little Trolls caught sight of the great white bear,

which all this time lay quiet and good under the stove. The little Troll found a piece of sausage and he stuck it on a fork.

"Pussy! Pussy! Will you have a bit of sausage?" he screamed as he poked the fork hard against the bear's tender black nose. Then he laughed and pulled it away again so that the bear couldn't get the sausage.

Then the great white bear was very angry. Up he rose and, with a growl like thunder, he came out from under the stove and, in a moment, he had chased the whole pack of Trolls out of the house.

So the hunter praised him and patted him and gave him a big bit of sausage to eat in his place under the stove. Then he called Halvor and the family to come out of the woodshed. They were very surprised to find the Trolls gone, and they cleared up the mess while the hunter told them what had happened. Then they all sat down to eat what was left of their Christmas dinner.

The next day the hunter and the bear thanked Halvor and set out again on their long journey to the court of the King of Denmark.

Next year Halvor was out, just about sunset, in a wood at the edge of

the Dovrafell on the afternoon of Christmas Eve. He was busy cutting all the wood they would want for the holiday. When he stopped to rest for a moment, leaning on his ax, he heard a voice that seemed to come from far away on the other side of the wood.

"Halvor! Halvor!" someone was shouting and calling.

"What do you want?" shouted Halvor. "Here I am."

"Have you got your big white cat with you still?" called the voice.

"Yes, that I have!" called back Halvor. "She's lying at home under the stove this moment. What's more, she has got seven kittens now, each bigger and fiercer than she is herself!"

"Then we'll never come to see you again!" bawled out the Troll from the other side of the wood.

What's more he never did, and so, since that time, the Trolls of the Dovrafell have never eaten their Christmas dinner at Halvor's house again.

A Norse tale

Childe Rowland

ONCE UPON A TIME, long ago, there was a queen in England and she had three bold sons and one fair daughter.

One evening the three Princes and Burd Ellen, their sister, were out playing with their golden ball and, as they played, the youngest son, Childe Rowland, sent the ball up so hard that it flew over the church roof.

Off ran their sister, Burd Ellen, to fetch the ball back again. The three Princes waited, but Burd Ellen neither came nor called. Then they went to find her but, search as they would, call as they would, there was no sign of her nor of the ball, and their hearts grew heavy, for they feared that she must have fallen into some evil enchantment.

So, at last, after they had sought her east, and sought her west, and all in vain, and when the Queen, their mother, could do no more but sit on her golden throne and weep, the eldest brother said that he would go and ask the advice of Merlin, the most famous of all the Enchanters of Britain.

So out he set, and when he got to the Enchanter's cave he told Merlin the whole tale – how they four had been playing with their golden ball and how Childe Rowland, the youngest Prince, had sent it high over the church roof, and how their sister, Burd Ellen, had run round calling out to them that she would fetch it back, and how no one had seen her since that day. Then he asked the Enchanter if he could tell what had become of her. Merlin asked the Prince which way round Burd Ellen had run. And when the Prince had answered, Merlin nodded his head.

"Burd Ellen," said Merlin, "has fallen under an enchantment because she went round the church 'widdershins,' that is, the contrary way to the sun. By my art I know that the King of Elfland has carried her off and that he has taken her to his Dark Tower. Hard will it be to win her back."

"If it is possible – if it is a thing that mortal man may do," said the Prince, "I will try."

"Possible it is," replied Merlin, "but woe to any man that tries unless he is well taught beforehand! Boldness is not all!"

Then the eldest Prince begged Merlin to tell him what he must do and what he must not do. Then, after Merlin had taught him, and after he had repeated his lesson, the eldest Prince said farewell to the Queen and his two brothers and rode off on the road to Elfland.

> *But long they waited, and longer still,*
> *With muckle doubt and pain,*
> *And woe were the hearts of his brethren,*
> *For he came not back again.*

After many days had passed, the second brother said that he would try, and he went to the Enchanter Merlin and asked his help to get his sister back again, just as his brother had done. He was given the very same teaching as to how a mortal man might win her back and off he set to ride to Elfland.

> *But long they waited, and longer still,*
> *With muckle doubt and pain,*
> *And woe were his mother's and brother's hearts,*
> *For he came not back again.*

At last, after many days, Childe Rowland, the youngest Prince, wanted to go, so he went to his mother, the good Queen, to ask her blessing. But at first, she would not let him go, for he was the last of her children and if he were lost, all would be lost.

But he begged so long that at last the Queen said he might go and since he was their last hope, she gave him his father's good sword that never struck in vain. As she buckled the sword belt round his waist, the Queen said the spell that would give the sword victory and then, as his brothers had done, Childe Rowland rode to Merlin's enchanted cave.

"Once more! And but once more, we come to you!" said Childe Rowland, when he stood before Merlin. "Tell me how a mortal man may rescue the fair Burd Ellen and my two brothers."

Merlin taught him as he had taught his brothers:

"My son," said he, "there are two things, simple they seem, but hard they are to do. One is something that you must do, and one is something you must not do. The thing you must do is this. After you have entered the Kingdom of Elfland, whoever speaks to you, till you see the fair Burd Ellen, you must out with your sword and you must cut off his head. The other is the thing you must not do. However hungry or thirsty you may be, you must drink no drop, nor eat one bite of food while you are in Elfland. If you do, you will never see Middle Earth again!"

Then Merlin told him how he must set out to find Elfland and the

Dark Tower, and that it was the Elf King himself who must be forced to tell him what had become of his two brothers.

Childe Rowland thanked the Enchanter and rode out on the way that his two brothers had ridden and that Merlin had told him.

He went and he went, till at last he came to where a horseherd was sitting with many horses feeding all round him. Childe Rowland could see by their wildness and their fiery eyes that these must be horses of Elfland.

"Can you tell me," said Childe Rowland to the horseherd, "where to find the Dark Tower of the King of Elfland?"

"I cannot tell," said the horseherd, "but go on a little farther and you will see a cowherd. Maybe he can tell you."

Then, without a word more, Childe Rowland drew his father's good sword that never struck in vain and off went the horseherd's head. Childe Rowland went on farther till he came to the cowherd and he asked him the same question.

"I cannot tell," said the cowherd, "but go on a little farther and you will come to the hen-wife. She is sure to know."

Then, once more, Childe Rowland drew the good sword that never struck in vain, and off went the cowherd's head. At last he came to an old woman in a gray cloak, and he asked her if she knew where the Dark Tower of the King of Elfland might be.

"Go on a little farther," said the hen-wife, "till you come to a steep, round hill. You must go round it three times widdershins, and, as you go, you must say:

> *Open, door! Open, door!*
> *And let me come in.*

The third time the door will open, and you may go in."

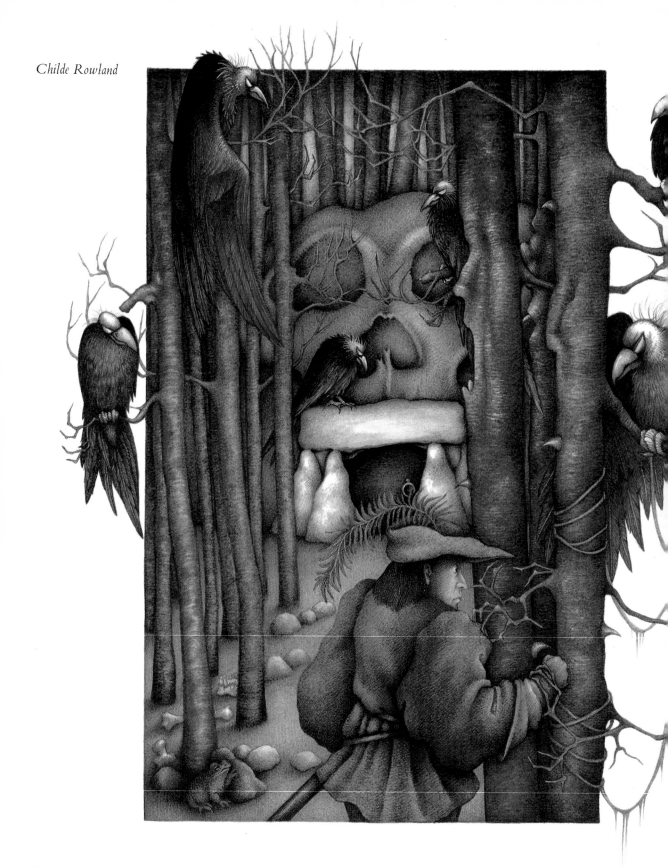

Childe Rowland

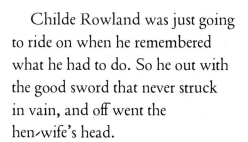

Childe Rowland was just going to ride on when he remembered what he had to do. So he out with the good sword that never struck in vain, and off went the hen-wife's head.

On he rode till at last he came to a round, green hill, and when he saw that, he jumped off his horse. There was a narrow door in the side of it, but it was fast shut. He went round the green hill on foot, widdershins, and as he went he said:

"Open, door! Open, door!
And let me come in."

Twice he did this and nothing happened. The door was still fast. But the third time the door opened and Childe Rowland went in.

Then the door shut again and Childe Rowland was alone.

It was not exactly dark. There was a kind of twilight or gloaming, and he seemed to be in a passage that was only just wide enough for him to pass. There were neither windows nor lamps and he could not tell where the soft light came from, unless it were through the walls and roof, which seemed to be made of transparent rock. The air was warm, as it always is in Elfland.

He went along softly till he saw, at the end of this passage, two wide, high doors and when he pushed on boldly and opened them, he saw a wonderful and glorious sight.

Before him was a large and high hall, as high as a great church. The pillars were all of gold and silver, and round their tops were wreaths of flowers made of diamonds and emeralds and all manner of precious stones. From the very middle of the high roof there hung, by a chain, a huge lamp made out of what seemed to be a great pearl all hollowed out. In the very middle of the pearl was a huge red carbuncle and this gave light to the whole hall.

Far off, at the end of the room, stood a beautiful couch of silk and gold and there, on the couch, whom should he see sitting but his sister, the fair Burd Ellen, combing her golden hair with a silver comb. When she saw Childe Rowland she stood up and her face was full of fear and sorrow as she spoke to him:

> *"God pity you, poor luckless fool,*
> *What have you here to do?*
> *Hear you this, my youngest brother,*
> *Why didn't you bide at home?*
> *Had you a hundred thousand lives*
> *You couldn't spare any a one.*
>
> *But sit you down; but woe, O, woe,*
> *That ever you were born,*
> *For come the King of Elfland in,*
> *Your fortune is forlorn."*

But Childe Rowland greeted her kindly and embraced her and told her why he had come. When they had sat down together, Childe Rowland asked for news of their two brothers. She wept as she told him how first one and then the other had reached the Dark Tower, but how, in the end, they had been enchanted by the King of Elfland, and now each lay in a stone coffin as if dead.

After they had talked a little, Childe Rowland began to feel faint and hungry from his long travels, and then, forgetting all about Merlin's warning, he begged his sister to give him a little food. At that Burd Ellen looked at him sadly, and shook her head, but because she was under a spell, she could do no more by way of warning. Instead, she was obliged to rise, and go out and soon she brought back a golden basin full of bread and milk. Childe Rowland was just going to raise it to his lips, when, catching sight of the sad face of his sister, he remembered just in time, and suddenly dashed bowl and all to the ground, saying:

"Not a sup will I swallow, not a bit will I bite, till Burd Ellen is free."

Just as he spoke they heard the noise of heavy footsteps and soon a loud voice crying:

"Fee, fi, fo, fum,
I smell the blood of a Christian man,

Be he alive or be he dead,
I'll dash his brains from his brainpan."

With that, the great doors of the hall burst open, and in rushed the terrible King of Elfland with his drawn sword flashing in his hand. But Childe Rowland was not afraid, for he stood ready with his sword.

"Strike then, Bogle, if you dare!" he shouted and rushed to meet the Elf King.

They fought. For long they fought. Sometimes one seemed to be winning and sometimes the other, but at last Childe Rowland had beaten the King of Elfland down on to his knees and, as he stood over him with his raised sword, the Elf King begged for mercy.

"I will give you mercy, and spare your life," said Childe Rowland, "if you swear to release my sister from your spells. Then you must raise my brothers to life, and, after all that is done, you must let us all go out free from your Dark Tower."

The beaten Bogle had to agree to this, so Childe Rowland let him get up. Then the Elf King went to a strong chest, and from it he took a little crystal bottle filled with something blood-red. Then Childe Rowland was taken to where his two brothers lay as if dead in their stone coffins.

But now, with his red salve, the Elf King touched their ears, eyelids, nostrils, lips and fingertips. No sooner had he done this than they sprang up, as well as ever they had been, and told Childe Rowland that their souls had been far away, but had now come back to them. Next the Elf King said

some words over Burd Ellen and the spell was taken off her too. And then he gave the little crystal bottle of salve to Childe Rowland. So, at last, they all passed out of the splendid hall of the defeated Elf King. Through the long passage they went and out of the door, which opened at their touch but shut again behind them. Glad they were to see wholesome daylight again and to turn their backs on the Dark Tower.

Then, as they went on their homeward way rejoicing, Childe Rowland remembered the hen-wife, the cowherd and the horseherd. There they lay, all three, where he had left them, but with a touch of the red salve, Childe Rowland was able to restore them to life.

When at last they all reached home, the good Queen their mother laughed for joy, and she ordered a great feast, so that everyone, great and small, in the whole kingdom, should be able to rejoice with her, because the fair Burd Ellen and her three brothers were safe home again.

An English tale

The King, the Saint and the Goose

DID YOU EVER HEAR what happened to good King O'Toole, who lived long ago in Ireland, and how it was that his old age was made pleasant to him?

If you never heard it, isn't it high time you did?

Now, in his young days, King O'Toole had been one of the finest young fellows in all Ireland. He loved hunting better than anything in the world, and from the rising of the sun till darkness came, he would be out galloping and hallooing with his horse and his hounds.

This went on merrily for a long while, but in the end the King grew too old and too stiff to be hunting all day, summer and winter, be it wet or be it fine. Indeed, a winter came when it was as much as the poor old

King could do to hobble about with a stick or even a crutch. Why, then it's lost he was, for he felt as if there wasn't any amusement or diversion

left for him in the world.

So at last, what did that poor old King do, but tame a wild goose to

amuse and divert him. You may
laugh, but she was a very good,
faithful creature was that goose.

For a while they had a lot of
pleasure together, her and King
O'Toole. She would fly round and
about, but would always come back
when he called her and would
waddle after him if that was what
would please him. On a Friday
(that, you know, is a fast day) she
would swim far out into the lake,
two or three times, and come back
each time to him with a nice plump
trout for his dinner.

So that good creature was

all poor old King O'Toole's
amusement and pleasure. But my
dear! The sadness of the world! The
time came when the poor old goose
grew too old too, and one winter the
truth was that she was as stiff in the
wing as her master was in the leg, so
that, try as she would, the poor
faithful creature couldn't amuse him
any more. Why then, the old King
was lost entirely and had no more
pleasure in life.

One day these two distressful creatures were sitting by the side of the lake. The King had his poor old goose in his arms, and he was looking down fondly at her, the tears in his eyes, lamenting because neither he nor she had any more pleasure. Then, presently, he let her go and she waddled off to get a bite to eat. But the old King sat on, thinking that he might as well be dead and drowned in the lake, as live such a miserable and distressful life.

Then he happened to look up, and what should he see standing before him but a decent young fellow that seemed to be a stranger to those parts.

"God save you, King O'Toole," said the decent young fellow.

"How come you know my name?" says the King.

"Never mind for that!" answered the fellow. "I know a lot of what passes. And may I make bold to ask how is your goose, King O'Toole?"

"And how come you know about my goose?" asked the King (for, you see, she was out of sight now, among the weeds).

"I know all about her. No matter how," said the young fellow, smiling.

"And who may you be?" asked the King.

"An honest man," answered the fellow.

"And how do you get a living?" asked the King.

"By making old things as good as new."

"Is it a tinker you are then?" asked the King.

"No. I've got a better trade than that. What would you say, King O'Toole, if I were to offer to make your goose as good as new?"

"As good as new?" asked the King, and he smiled all over his poor old face, thinking that, of all the pleasures of this world, that would please him the best.

"Yes! As good as new," said the young fellow, nodding.

King O'Toole gave a whistle, and out of the reeds came his poor old goose, waddling and limping. As obedient as a hound she was, that creature, and faithful to her poor old crippled master. When the young man looked down and saw her he nodded again.

"Yes," says he, "I could do the job for you easy enough."

"By the holy word," says the King, looking down in his turn and seeing the poor old bag-of-bones of a goose, "if you can do that, why you're the cleverest young fellow in seven parishes!"

"I'm better than that, bedad," says the young man, laughing, "but what will you give me now, if I do the job for you?"

"I'll give you whatever you ask for," says the King. "Isn't that fair enough?"

"Will you give me all the ground the goose covers the first time she flies after she's been made as good as new?"

"Indeed I will," says the King.

"You'll not go back on your word?" says the young fellow.

"I will not," says the King.

Then the young man called to the poor bag-of-bones of a goose:

"You poor unhappy old cripple!" says he, catching her gently by the wings. "It's I that will make you a fine sporting bird again!" With that he made the sign of the cross over her and then he threw her up into the air and, as he threw her, he blew at her feathers just to give her a bit of a lift. Sakes alive! If that goose didn't fly off from his hand as if it was one of the eagles of the mountains that she was. Aye, and she sported and capered in the air with delight, just like any swallow.

It was a beautiful sight to see the old King, for he was there with his mouth open for joy and surprise, looking at his poor old goose, and she flying as light as a lark in the sky.

Well, she had a good fly round – out of sight and back again – then she lit down at her master's feet with a shake of her wings. When he had patted her head and stroked her all down her back he could tell that she was as good as, and even better than, ever she had been.

"Sure, you're the darling of the world," says the old King to the goose.

"And what do you say to me?" asked the young fellow.

"I say you're the cleverest fellow that walks the ground of Ireland," replied the King, still looking at his goose.

"No more than that?"

"I say I'll be grateful to you to my dying day."

"But will you do as you said and give me the land that the goose flew over just now?"

"I will," said the King, looking up at last. "You'd be welcome to it if it was the last acre I'd got."

"You're a good, decent old man, for you keep to a bargain," says the young fellow, "and well for you and your goose that you are, else your bird would never fly again!"

"But who are you?" asked the King for the second time that morning, for he seemed to see a change coming over the young fellow.

"I'm Saint Kevin," he answered.

"Oh, Queen of Heaven!" said the King, making the sign of the cross, and dropping to his knees as well as he could for the stiffness of his joints. "And is it with a holy saint I've been speaking and discoursing all this while?"

"It is," said Saint Kevin.

"And me thinking it was only a decent young lad!"

"I came in disguise," said the saint, "so how would you be knowing with whom you were talking and discoursing; I came to try you, King O'Toole, and I've been finding this morning that you're a decent old King, for it seems that you'll keep a bargain even with one you took to be no more than a tinker."

Well, King O'Toole had kept his bargain, so sure enough he had his goose as good as new to amuse and divert him till the day he died, and though 'twas only a little bit of a kingdom that he had left, the saint

evermore provided for the two of them — for the King and the goose.

So now you know how it came about that all that queer-shaped bit of ground in that part of Ireland belongs to one of the saints of Heaven.

An Irish tale

The Country of
The Mice

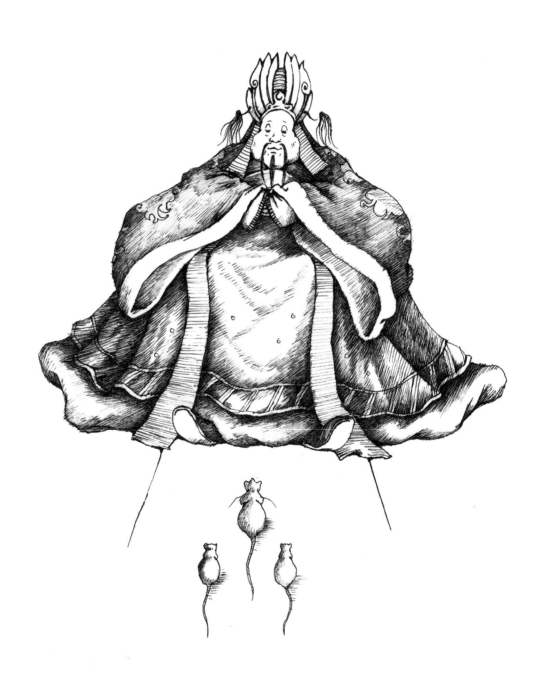

THERE WAS ONCE a part of Tibet where there were two strange laws. The first of these was that no one, on pain of death, might keep a cat. The second was that in a certain valley – down which ran a big mountain stream – the monks of the nearby monastery must keep the stone embankment on their side in good repair. These two laws were made for a very special reason and if you read on you will know what that reason was.

The man who was, long ago, the King of this part of Tibet was an excellent man. One day, as he was sitting on his throne in the inner courtyard of his palace, he was told that a very grandly dressed mouse, with a number of attendant mice, was at the gate, and that the grand mouse was asking to see him.

The King was very much amused at the idea of having a visit from a talking mouse and he gave orders that this splendid fellow and his attendants were to be brought in at once.

Now it is the custom in Tibet for all visitors – at any rate on great occasions – to bring with them a present of a white silk scarf. The King was delighted to see that, when he came before the throne, the mouse knew all about this custom, and that he brought, not exactly a scarf, but a beautiful single thread of white silk. The silk thread was handed by one of the mouse's attendants to one of the King's guards, with a low bow.

The King now politely bade the mouse welcome and soon the visitor was explaining why he had come.

"O King," began the mouse, "you must know that this year our harvest was bad, our crops have fallen short, and we are threatened with hunger and famine unless we can borrow enough grain to carry us through the winter. So I, who am ruler and chief of all the mice of your country, stand before you here to ask if you can help us. If you can lend us what barley and oats we need, we will not only pay you back faithfully at our next harvest, but, as interest, with more grain than you lend us."

"Very well," agreed the King. "How much do you want?"

"I think," said the mouse, "that we shall need about one of your big barns full."

"Good gracious!" said the King, astonished. "And if I really do lend you a whole barnful of grain, how in the world do you think you could ever carry it away?"

"Leave that to me!" replied the mouse in a confident tone. "If you will consent to lend the grain, we will do the rest."

So the King agreed to lend the mice one of his great granaries full of barley and oats. He decided on the largest and ordered his officers to throw open its doors, and to let the mice carry away as much as they wanted.

That night, the chief and ruler of the mice summoned his subjects together, and, to the number of many hundred of thousands, they came to the barn. Then each mouse picked up as much grain as he could carry. One mouse would hold it in his mouth, another in a tiny sack on his back, and others had some curious way of carrying it curled up in their tails. They made a very tidy job of it and when they had finished, the barn was completely empty, and not a single grain of barley or oats was left behind.

Next morning, when the King went out to look at his barn, he was very much astonished to find that the mice really had been able to take the grain away so quickly, and he began to have a very high opinion of them.

"These are very efficient mice," said he to his courtiers.

When, after the next harvest, the chief and ruler of the mice kept his

promise and paid back the grain with interest, the King decided that the mice were honest as well as clever.

Now it happened, not long after this, that the country over which this King ruled was attacked by the ruler of a neighboring kingdom. This kingdom lay on the opposite side of the big mountain and river, and was far richer and more powerful than the country where the mice lived. Soon a large army was on the march and ready to attack.

When the mice heard what was happening they were very worried, for they feared that, if the enemy entered their country and dethroned the King who had been their friend over the loan of the grain, they themselves might not be so well off. In fact, they did not like the idea of a strange ruler.

So the mouse put on his grandest robes, and, with his attendants, set out to visit the King again. When he got to the palace he again asked for an interview with his majesty. He was shown in at once, and once more offered a single thread instead of the usual scarf. Finding that the King was looking very depressed, the mouse chief spoke at once in a grand but squeaky manner:

"I have come to you a second time, O King, in order to see whether I can be of use to you. The last time I was here you did me and my people a great favor, and if it is now in our power to help in any way, we shall be very glad to do our best."

In spite of feeling depressed about the war, the King could not but feel amused to hear such solemn words from a mouse.

"I thank you very much," said he, "but really what could your excellent mice do to help? We are threatened with invasion by a foreign army, outnumbering mine by many thousands. This army is already encamped just across the river. All the men I can muster will not be enough to prevent them from crossing as soon as they choose. Thank you yet again, but I don't see how mice could help."

"Do you remember, O King," replied the mouse in a calm tone, "that on the first occasion I was here you did not believe that we should be able to carry away the grain you had lent us, or to pay back the loan? And yet we proved ourselves able to do both! All we ask you now is to trust us again, and, if you will undertake to do one or two things which we will ask of you, we, on our part, will undertake to rid you of the invading army."

The King was very interested, and he replied:

"Very well, mouse. What you say is true. I didn't believe last time you would be able to do what you said but I trusted you and I will trust you again. Tell me now what you wish my servants or my army to do, and I will see that they carry out our share of the bargain."

"Very good," answered the mouse. "All we wish you to do is provide us, by tomorrow evening, with one hundred thousand sticks. Each stick must be about a foot long, and they must all be laid neatly in rows on the bank of the river. If you will undertake to do this, we on our side will undertake to put the opposing army in a state of confusion and panic! But I should like to add something more. If we succeed in doing all we promise, we shall, later, ask you to safeguard us against the two

principal dangers which threaten our existence."

"If you can really do what you say," replied the King, "I will certainly try to safeguard you against these dangers, if you tell me what they are."

"The dangers to which I refer," answered the mouse, "are, gracious King, the dangers of floods and cats. Most of our mouse-holes – our homes – are in the low-lying land near the river, and whenever the snows melt and the river rises, it overflows this level country and floods our holes and nests. What we would suggest to your majesty, is that you should build a strong wall – an embankment – all along the river, so as to make sure that the water cannot overflow into our homes. As to cats, they are always the persecutors of mice, and we ask you to banish all cats forever from your kingdom."

"Very well," replied the King, "if you succeed in getting rid of the large and powerful army which now threatens us, I will undertake to do what you ask."

On hearing this the mouse chief bowed low to the King, and, after making polite farewells, he went back as fast as he could to his own subjects.

Next morning, early, he sent out messengers to call together all the

full-grown mice of his kingdom, and, when they came, he gave them his orders. About dusk he was able to lead a large army, numbering several hundreds of thousands of mice, to the bank of the river, where he found the sticks all neatly laid out exactly as the King had promised.

The mice had fully understood the orders they had been given, and each small group at once proceeded to launch a stick on the river, by means of which they soon crossed over to the other side.

It was quite dark by the time they got across and the enemy soldiers were all asleep in their camp. Some were lying in tents and some were lying outside in blankets, but all had their weapons beside them ready for any alarm. But no alarm was given. The mice were soundless. They did not even need a word of command from their chief, but at once scattered themselves through the camp, whereupon each one began to do as much damage as he

possibly could in the shortest possible time.

Some went to the bowmen and nibbled their bowstrings. Some went to where the musketeers were sleeping and gnawed through their musket slings. Others bit holes in the clothes of the men and some bit off their pigtails. Others bit holes in

sacks so that everything in them spilled.

In fact, these bold mice attacked anything upon which their teeth could make an impression, so that tents, stores, grain, and provisions of all kinds were soon in shreds or scattered in confusion.

After a couple of hours of such silent work the chief collected his mouse army on the river bank, and, embarked on their stick-rafts once more, they paddled themselves quietly over to their own shore without a sound having been heard by the enemy.

But next morning, at daybreak, when the enemy soldiers began to stir, there was a fearful outcry in the camp. Each man as he woke from sleep found himself in a woeful state – his clothes in rags, his pigtail nibbled, his bowstring gnawed, his musket without a sling to carry it or a fuse to light it. What was almost worse – there was nothing to eat for breakfast! No – not a single crumb! Each soldier at once began to accuse the other of theft and treachery. Before many minutes had passed the whole camp was in uproar, comrade quarreling with comrade, and every man in the field was accusing the other.

The mouse ruler had, of course, advised the King that now was the time for the King's small army to attack. He did not actually do more than march down to the river, but

he flew the great flag in the blue sky
and had the great drum beaten on
the terrace of the palace. So, in the
middle of their confusion, the enemy soldiers on the
opposite bank saw the flag and heard the great drum
and, terrified at the thought of having to fight in their
present confusion, the whole enemy army took flight.

As for the mice, safe from floods and cats, they
lived happily, and every year the King also provided for them a gift of
grain in thankful recognition of the splendid help they had given him in
time of need.

The King naturally wanted to make quite sure that there would not
be any more invasions. What he did, after thanking the mice, was to
send a herald across the river to the enemy capital. The herald was told to
say that, on this occasion, the King had only considered it worthwhile to
employ a few mice to defeat his enemies. But if he was ever threatened
again, he would be ready to beat back the attack first with all his cows,
sheep, yaks, cats and dogs; and if they did not succeed, he would order
out mountain tigers, wild dogs, wolves and bears, and if they failed, he
would come out to war himself with all his warriors!

When the foreign ruler heard this message he was very frightened and
considered it wiser at once to make a treaty of peace.

"How," he said to himself, "can I hope to defeat even

53

the tame animals, let alone the wild beasts and the soldiers, of a country whose mice can show such skill and courage?"

So peace was made and the two countries remained on friendly terms for many years after.

A Tibetan tale

The Well of
the World's End

LONG AGO, in a lonely cottage, a girl lived
with her mother, who was a widow woman. One
day the widow gave her a sieve and told her to go and fill it with water
from the Well of the World's End. "And," said she, "mind you bring it
home to me full."

At that the girl was very sad, and taking the sieve she started off with a
heavy heart. As she went she asked everyone she met where the Well of
the World's End might be. But nobody knew, and she couldn't tell
what to do. However, she went, and she went, and at last she met a queer
old woman, all bent double, and the girl asked her too.

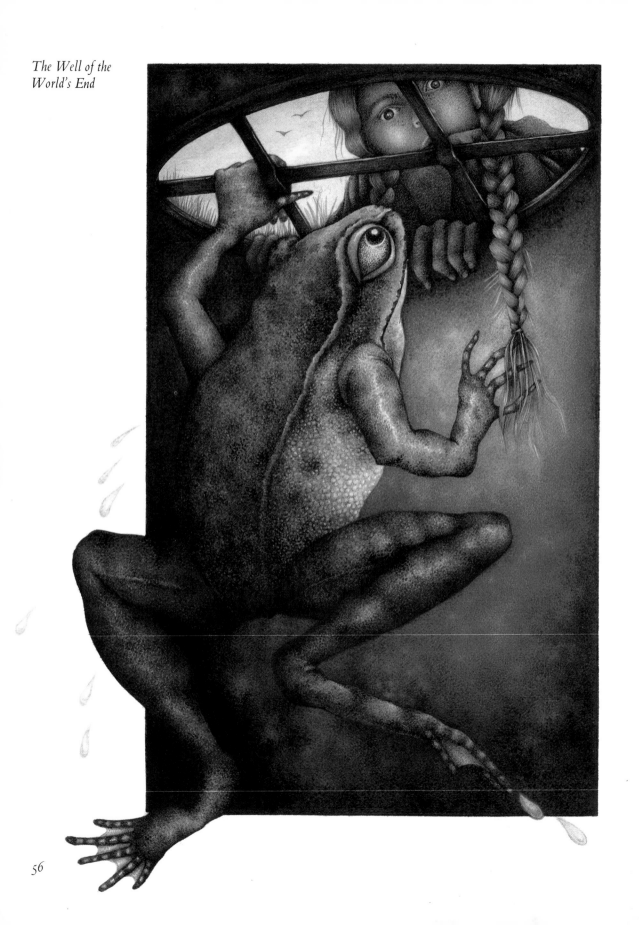

"Can you tell me, please," said she, "where is the Well of the World's End?"

The old woman answered her kindly and told her just where to find it, and how she was to go to get to it. So the girl thanked her, did just as the old woman said and, sure enough, she did find the well.

But dear, dear, her troubles were not ended yet for, as you can guess, when the girl dipped the sieve into the cold, cold well the water all ran out again. The girl tried and she tried, but it was no use, so at last she sat down on the edge of the well and she cried as if her heart would break.

Suddenly she heard a strange croaking voice:

"What is the matter, my dear?" said the voice, and with that she looked up. There sat a great frog, with large round eyes, looking at her.

"Matter enough!" said the girl, still crying, and then she told the frog how hard it had been to find the well and what her mother had said, and how, every time she dipped the sieve in the well, all the water ran out.

"If you promise," said the frog, "to do whatever I tell you for a whole night long, I'll help you. I'll tell you how to fill your sieve with the water from the Well of the World's End."

The girl thought the frog seemed friendly enough.

"And what harm can a frog do me, anyhow?" she thought. So she agreed, and then the frog said in its strange croaking voice:

> *"Stuff it with moss and daub it with clay*
> *And then it will carry the water away."*

No sooner had it said the last word than it gave a jump, and *plop*, *splash*, it disappeared into the cold, dark water of the Well of the World's End.

So the girl did just as the frog had told her. She found some moss and stuffed it between the holes in the sieve, and then she found some clay and she daubed it on the moss very carefully. Then she let it all dry a bit in the sun, and at last, once more, she dipped the sieve into the cold, cold waters of the well. This time the water did not run out and, with a light heart, the girl started off home. As she went she turned to have a last look at the Well of the World's End and, as she looked, the frog popped his head out of the well and he said:

"Remember your promise." The girl nodded.

"All right," she said, and she thought again, "What harm can a frog do me?"

So back she went and, this time, the way didn't see long at all and she brought the sieve full of water to her mother.

That very evening, as the two of them sat by the fire, they heard something tapping at the door, low down, and a voice said:

> *"Open the door, my honey, my heart,*
> *Open the door, my own darling;*
> *Mind you the words that you and I spoke,*
> *Down at the World's End Well."*

As you can guess, the mother was surprised to hear that. But the girl knew well enough who was at the door, and so she told her mother all about it.

"You must keep your promise, girl," said the mother. "Go and open the door."

So the girl got up, and she opened the door, and, sure enough, there was the great frog on the doorstep, and it was so wet that the water ran off the stone and down the path. It gave a hop right into the room and right up to the girl's feet, and when she took a step back to her chair, it took another big hop after her. It looked up at her with its great round eyes and said:

> *"Lift me to your knee, my honey, my heart,*
> *Lift me to your knee, my own darling;*
> *Remember the words that you and I spoke,*
> *Down by the World's End Well."*

As you can guess, the girl didn't much like the idea of that, for, as you know, the frog was dripping wet. But her mother said:

"Girls must keep their promises." At that the girl sat by the fire again and she lifted the frog on to her lap, and it was so wet that her apron and her dress were both soaked through in a moment, and it was so cold that it seemed to the girl as if the fire gave no heat.

For a long while the frog said never a word, but at last it spoke again:

> *"Give me some supper, my honey, my heart,*
> *Give me some supper, my darling;*
> *Remember the words that you and I spoke,*
> *Down by the World's End Well."*

The girl was glad enough to do that, so she got up and sat the frog on the chair, but the frog was so wet the water ran down to the floor. The girl made ready a bowl of bread and milk, and she fed the frog with a spoon, and when it had finished, it said:

> *"Go with me to bed, my honey, my heart,*
> *Go with me to bed, my own darling;*
> *Mind you the words you spoke to me,*
> *Down by the cold well, so weary."*

Well, the girl did not want to do that. She did not want to take the cold wet frog into her bed, but her mother said again:

"Girls must keep their promises." So sadly and sorrowfully, the girl took the frog with her to bed and, as you can guess, she kept it as far away from her as she could, and it is little sleep she got that night. Well, just as dawn was breaking she heard the frog speaking again, and this is what it said:

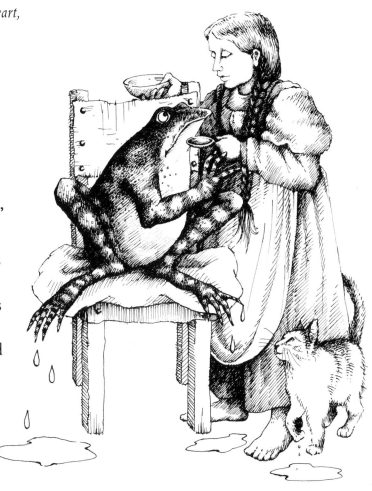

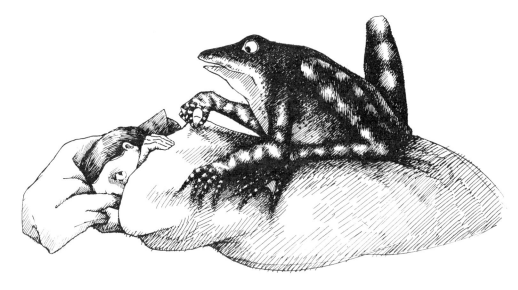

> *"Chop off my head, my honey, my heart,*
> *Chop off my head, my own darling;*
> *Remember the promise you made to me,*
> *Down by the cold well, so weary."*

Well, the girl was very sorry to hear the frog say that, for she remembered how it had been kind to her and how it had taught her to fill the sieve with water and, wet and cold though it was, she thought now that it was quite a pretty creature.

But the frog said again in its queer croaking voice:

> *"Chop off my head, my honey, my heart,*
> *Chop off my head, my own darling;*
> *Remember the promise you made to me,*
> *Down by the cold well, so weary."*

When she still didn't want to do it, the frog repeated the words a third time. So the girl saw there was no help for it. She went and found the ax, and she put the frog on the floor, and with tears running from her eyes she chopped off its head.

Then what do you think happened? There in front of her, instead of the frog, stood a handsome young prince, and he didn't speak with a frog's croaking voice anymore, but with his own clear voice. He took the girl by the hand and he told her that he had been enchanted by a wicked witch and that now the girl had broken the spell for him, for the spell was that in his frog state, he had to find a girl who would do his bidding for a whole night.

So they were married and they went to live in the castle of the King, his father. There was great rejoicing because now the spell was off, and he was a prince again, and they lived happily ever after.

An English tale

The Magic Bird

*Hear my tale! What happened did not happen in my village,
nor did it happen in your village.
All the same it was in Africa that it happened.*

THE TRIBE that lived in this village didn't have any cattle. No!
They grew kaffir-corn and groundnuts and maize and such crops
as that in their gardens and fields. Now and then they traded the things
they could grow with the people of other tribes who kept cows. Unless
they did this they never had a chance to taste milk, or curds and whey, or
butter, or cream, though they liked these things just as much as you do,
and as I do. Sometimes they managed to grow very good crops in their
clearings, but that didn't always happen and, as I've told you, there were
no cows at all. No cows!

One year the crops were really bad, so all the people of the tribe
thought that they would try fresh ground and go hoeing and sowing in a
place that had never been gardened before. So that's what they did, they
all went off to work on new ground.

One of the men who went was called Masilo. His wife and their two
children, who were called Duma and Dumasine – a boy and a girl –
went with him. The first thing that Masilo did when they got to the new
garden strip was to make a little branch shelter, a sort of small green hut
to rest in for an hour at noon in the great heat, and then, for the rest of
the day, he and his wife and the two children worked at clearing the
ground of weeds and stones. After that they hoed it, ready to put in
the seed.

That evening, when the sun began to get low and it was time for
everyone to go back to the village, Masilo and his wife and children went
back with the rest. They all walked along the path with their hoes over
their shoulders.

But then, what do you think? As soon as everyone was out of sight, a
beautiful bird flew down and came and sat on the roof of the little shelter
that Masilo had built, and as soon as it had perched it began to whistle
and sing. The tune was nice enough, but oh dear! What sort of words
did that pretty bird sing?

> *"Chanchassa Chanchassa Kilhiso!*
> *Ground, put yourself back!*
> *Be as you were,*
> *Strip that was hoed by Masilo!"*

Could you believe it, my children? That was exactly what the strip did.
All the weeds that had been there blew back or rolled back, and took
root again, and all the grass sods and the stones that they had worked so
hard to hoe up, all put themselves back as well. The other people's
garden strips were all right, but it didn't look as if anyone had worked
on poor Masilo's strip at all.

Next morning, when Masilo and his wife and children came back
with the seed they couldn't believe their eyes.

"Can that really be the garden strip that we all cleared and hoed so
nicely yesterday?" they asked each other. "The strip that was all tidy and
ready for sowing?" But though they were terribly disappointed they could

see that it really was the same strip, because, you see, to the right and left of it, the very same neighbors who had worked alongside of them the day before were busy once more. Both lots of neighbors had brought their seeds, so now they could begin sowing because their strips were all right.

When the others looked up from their work and saw Masilo's ground they laughed:

"You really are a lazy lot, Masilo! You and your family are bone-idle – that's what's wrong!"

Well, Masilo and his wife were too miserable to answer back and thought that there was nothing for it but to try again. The sun was very hot but, in spite of that, they and the children worked all day and, by evening, they had once more got the whole strip ready for sowing. So, at last, very tired, off they all four went, home with the others.

But it was all no good! No sooner were they out of sight than the beautiful bird came back.

What a bird it was! Its wings were scarlet, its long tail was steely blue, it had patches of white that shone like silver on its back, and its pretty round head shone like gold. Once more it flew down to the top of Masilo's little shelter-hut, once more it began to whistle and sing. The tune was very pretty, but I am sorry to tell you, oh my children, the words were the same that it had sung before:

"Chanchassa Chanchassa Kilhiso!
Ground, put yourself back!

Be as you were,
Strip that was hoed by Masilo!"

And when the beautiful bird had done singing, that strip was as bad as ever again, and once more it looked as if no one had ever worked on it.

When Masilo and his wife and the two children came back next morning, they really were most bitterly disappointed. But what could they do? Again, all day, they worked in the hot sun. But then, something different happened. In the evening, when the sun was ready to set, Masilo said:

"Someone or something has bewitched this strip. Go home, wife, and take the children with you, and I'll stay here and see what sort of creature it can be that has spoiled all our work."

So his wife and the two children, Duma the boy, and Dumasine the girl, joined the long line of tired people who were all winding back along the narrow path to the village. But Masilo didn't go. He hid under the little branch shelter that he had built.

He hadn't long to wait. Soon he saw a most beautiful bird that flew down and perched itself on the roof of the shelter, just above the place where he was hidden. Such a beautiful bird Masilo had never seen. Its red and steely blue and silver shone in the setting sun and so did its golden head and, what's more, it seemed to be a most gay and cheerful bird. It hopped about, it flapped its scarlet wings, it spread its steel-blue tail, and then it began to whistle. The tune was pretty enough! But as soon as it began to sing, the third day's work was spoiled.

"Chanchassa Chanchassa Kilhiso!
Ground, put yourself back!
Be as you were,
Strip that was hoed by Masilo!"

Then Masilo, who was crouching just below it, hidden in the shelter, stretched up his hand through the loose branches and caught the bird by the legs. The creature flapped its scarlet wings and struggled and tried to get away, but Masilo held on tight.

"So it's YOU, you cruel bird, that's spoiled all our work! All the work that we'd done in the hot sun," cried Masilo. Then, still holding the bird's legs with one hand, he took out his big sheath-knife and got ready to cut its head off.

"Don't kill me!" said the bird. "I'll make you as much milk and curds and cream as ever you like!"

"YOU make milk and curds and cream? But you're a bird!" said Masilo.

"You'll soon see!" said the bird.

"I don't believe a word of it!" answered Masilo and then he hesitated. "But anyhow, before I really decide not to cut your head off, I shall have to have some sort of proof that you're really able to work good magic as well as bad."

"Watch this, then!" said the bird, and it sang these words but to another tune:

"Chanchassa Chanchassa Kilhiso!
Get yourself ready for sowing,
Ground that was hoed by Masilo!"

Would you believe it! In a minute, the strip was all ready for sowing
again. There wasn't a weed or stone on it.

Then Masilo, still holding onto the bird with one hand, put away the
sheath-knife and then picked a big leaf with the other hand and said:

"Now let's see if you can do what you boasted about! Let's see if you
can fill this leaf with milk or with curds and whey."

Do you know, oh my children, that that's just what the bird did?
It clapped its wings two or three times so quickly that Masilo couldn't
see exactly what it was doing. But what he did see was that the big leaf
was soon full of delicious curds and whey. Masilo was hungry and
thirsty and so, in case it all disappeared again, he swallowed it all up
at once.

So then he pulled an old sack out of the shelter and then started to
carry the bird off to his hut. But he didn't want anyone to see what he'd
got, so, before he came to the village, he put the bird in the sack.

When he was safe inside his house he carefully shut all the openings
and said to his wife:

"Wife! Wash out all the biggest pots that we've got, the ones that we
brew beer in!"

"What's the sense of doing that?" asked his wife. "We've got nothing
to put in them!"

"Just you listen to me!" answered Masilo. "Just do what I ask you!
Then you'll see!"

So the wife did as her husband asked, and she cleaned out all the big
beer crocks and pots. Then Masilo told the two children to go outside
and, when they'd gone, he pulled the bird out of the sack.

"Now, you bird you! Fill all those crocks and pots with milk or curds
or cream! Don't forget that you spoiled three days' work on our strip, so
give us plenty or it'll be the worse for you."

The bird began to spread its wings and tail and dance about and clap its wings and, sure enough, in another moment, all those big pots and crocks were full of delicious milk or curds or cream.

When all this was done, Masilo put the bird back in the sack, hid it, and called the children. Then they all sat down and had the best meal they'd had for a long time.

"Now remember," said Masilo to his children, Duma and Dumasine, "don't you tell anybody what sort of a supper you had tonight! Be sure not to tell the other children."

No indeed, they said, they'd never tell a word.

This went on for a long time. They always had a good supper when they got back tired from the garden strip, so Masilo and his wife and the two children got so fat and sleek that people were surprised to see how plump and well they looked.

"Why," they said, "is everybody in Masilo's house so fat? He has always been very poor. But now, already, since he made that new garden, though the crops aren't ripe enough to eat yet, all the same he and his wife and two children are so fat you could roll them down the hill!"

The neighbors tried their best to look into Masilo's hut because they hoped to see what it was they were getting to eat, but in vain.

Then, one morning, Masilo and his wife went with the others to work in their garden as usual. This time, however, the children didn't go with them. All the children in the village went out to play instead.

The others said to Masilo's children:

"Oh, Duma and Dumasine! Tell us how it is that while we're so thin, you're so fat?"

"Are we fat?" asked Duma and Dumasine. "We thought we were just as thin as you are!"

The two children answered like that, you see, because they didn't want to say anything about *why* it was that they had such sleek, shiny black skins. But the other children weren't going to be content with nonsense like that.

"Of course you're fatter than we are!" they said. "Oh, do, oh, do tell us the secret! We won't tell anyone else! We won't tell any of the grown-ups."

"All right," said Duma and Dumasine at last. "We'll tell you! In our father's house there's a bird that makes milk. It makes milk come into all the pots and crocks that we used to use for making beer and we get curds and cream as well as milk."

But of course the other children wouldn't believe them.

"How could a bird make milk come?" they said.

"We'll show you!" said Duma and Dumasine at last.

So into the hut they all went, and Masilo's two children pulled the bird out of the secret place where their father had hidden it. Then they did just as they had seen their father do, and soon the beautiful bird, with a cord round one leg, stood in the middle of the hut tied to a big stool. it danced about and waved and clapped its scarlet wings and spread its steel-blue tail and, in a moment, all the pots and all the crocks in the hut were full of milk and cream and curds.

"Help yourselves!" cried Duma and Dumasine proudly. Soon all the children were having a splendid time feasting, for they were all hungry, every one of them, and they knew that at home there wouldn't be much supper – not till the next crops were ready.

After they had feasted they all admired and stroked the beautiful bird. At last one of the children said:

"I believe that this bird could dance even better if we untied it. It doesn't like the cord – but just look at its lovely feathers!"

So the children did untie it and it danced in the middle of the hut while all the children clapped in time to its dancing. After a while the bird said:

"There isn't really room to dance properly here. Why not take me outside?"

So the children carried the bird outside and they all stood round it laughing and singing and dancing, while the bird danced in the middle,

bending its golden head, spreading its steel-blue tail and flapping its beautiful scarlet wings.

But oh, my children! Can you guess what happened? I expect you can! After quite a short time the bird flew right out of the circle of children and perched high on a treetop, well out of reach, and there it sat, as cheerful as could be, whistling its tune. Goodness, weren't the children frightened then! Masilo's boy and girl, Duma and Dumasine, were the most frightened of all and the girl cried:

"We *must* try and catch it! Our father will be very, very angry!"

So the whole lot of children set off after it. And do you know what the bird did? It led them on.

First it would fly for a short way, then it would hop and flutter

as if it couldn't fly anymore and then it would stand quite still. But as soon as a child got near enough to pounce, off it flew again.

Well, after a while the neighbors' children had had enough of it and went home, but Masilo's children – Duma and Dumasine – decided they must keep trying to get the bird back. So they kept on going a little farther and a little farther, always hoping that, next time, the bird would really stop and that they would be able to catch it.

At last evening came, and Masilo and his wife came back from their garden strip. But their hut was empty, there was no bird there, and no children. So they wondered what had happened. They minded most about the bird, for they thought the children were still out playing, so at first they didn't bother much about them but just felt sad and rather angry about the bird, and didn't know how they were ever going to have any more of the delicious cream and curds and whey. When evening came they began to get anxious about the children as well. They called and called. But no one seemed to know anything, because the neighbors' children, who knew quite a lot, never said a word.

As for Duma and Dumasine, when it began to get dark they thought they had better go back to

their parents even though they hadn't been able to catch the bird.

So what happened then? What happened then, oh my children, was a terrible storm with rain and thunder. It gradually got worse, and huge hailstones, big! big as pigeons' eggs, began to fall, so the two children sheltered under a big tree. The storm went on for a long time – all night – but at last with the first light it cleared and then Duma and Dumasine came out and, as they came out, they looked up at the tree.

They saw that this tree was covered with beautiful black fruits – rather like small black plums those fruits were – and they didn't seem to have been bruised by the storm. The children, who were very hungry by this time, each picked and ate a few that grew low enough to reach. And what do you think happened then? All the other plums, that were still growing on the tree, turned into little tiny birds that twittered and flew about. Then, in the middle of this cloud of tiny birds, they spied the magic bird.

Bright as a flower he was, and as cheerful as ever, spreading his scarlet wings, wagging his steel-blue tail up and down, whistling and dancing. The children hated the sight of him. At last the bird spoke:

"I suppose I'd better do something for you two children," said he. "After all, it was you who set me free!" So he bowed his beautiful golden head and snapped two little twigs off the tree. These he dropped down to

the children – one to each. "Go straight on," he said, "straight along this path till you come to a huge rock. Walk round it! Keep hitting the rock with these twigs! As you do this you must each call upon it to open:

Chanchassa Chanchassa Kilhiso!
I am the child of Masilo,
Open! Open!

That's what you must say! You must go on doing this if nothing happens at first. If you only do it often enough, a door in the rock will have to fly open. When it does, go through, for inside is a place where you can live until you are grown up."

The children took the twigs and started along the path. But they wondered if they would know which was the magic rock. Soon, however, there was no doubt about it, for they came in sight of an immense rock standing all by itself in the tall green grass, and the grass was the tallest and the rock the biggest that the children had ever seen. They walked round it calling out the words the bird had taught them:

"Chanchassa Chanchassa Kilhiso!
I am the child of Masilo,
Open! Open!"

Each time round they hit the rock with the magic twigs. Sure enough, after a time, a door in it did fly open and they looked in and saw that inside was a huge cave. This cave was more beautifully furnished than any hut they had ever seen. Oh, if only you could see it! It was so fine that a great chief or a king might have lived in it. There were finely plaited mats to sleep on, beautifully carved little wooden headrests for pillows, and splendid woven bedclothes and cloaks to keep the cold away in the day. There were bright shell and bead necklaces and girdles for Dumasine and, for each of them, a special cloak worked with beads. For Duma, there was a bow and arrows, there was a long, curly koodoo horn for him to blow, and beautiful small-sized throwing spears and assegais. All round the walls of this wonderful place stood pots and calabashes, each one dyed shining red and black. Some had cream in them, some had fresh milk and some curds, or else delicious porridge already cooked. Besides all this there were three big closely woven baskets. One was full of wheat, another was full of nuts, and a third full of maize. They went in and, when they had looked all round, the children both spoke together:

"This is the most beautiful place we have ever seen," they said. "Now we shall be quite happy!"

And there the two of them lived, till the boy had become a fine young man and Dumasine the prettiest young woman that you can imagine. There was always plenty to eat, for the calabashes filled up again as fast as Duma and Dumasine ate what was in them. They taught themselves to cook and keep house, and how to shoot the bow and arrows, blow the koodoo horn and throw the spears and assegais.

At last, one day, they found that their food stores were getting low. The calabashes and baskets were all gradually getting empty and not filling themselves up again.

75

"I know what it is. We are grown up now and it is time we worked for ourselves," said the girl.

"Yes, let us go out into the world," said the boy.

So they came out and after walking for many days they got back to the village where they had been born.

Their father and mother cried with joy when they saw that this fine young hunter and this lovely girl were none other than their lost Duma and Dumasine.

Every evening some of the people were sure to ask them to tell them their story – the very story that I've just told to you – and any stranger who came to the village was sure to want to hear

The Tale of the Magic Bird

There are many variations of this African story. In one version, after the magic bird's escape, there is the storm, but then all the children disappear in a "Pied Piper" incident. All, like Duma and Dumasine, are then thoughtfully looked after by various supernaturals, and return to their parents as adults.

The children's names in this version are Swazi and mean "Children of Thunder."

The Master-
Thief

LONG AGO, not in your day nor in my day, but in the very far-
off days, an old couple, who were very poor, lived in a little
tumbledown cottage. One day a splendid carriage with four black horses
drew up to their door. As soon as it stopped, a richly dressed young

gentleman greeted the old couple politely, and asked them if they would be so kind as to let him stay to dinner with them. He added that, if they would agree, he would pay them well. The old people looked at each other, and then the old man answered that they were only poor folk and that, as usual, they had no food in the house that was fit to set before the gentry. But the stranger said that that was just what he had hoped, and that if they had some potatoes that would be enough dinner for him, for he had a special fancy for potato-balls, but that none of the grand cooks in any of the towns through which he had traveled knew how to make such things properly. So the end of it was that the old wife went into the kitchen, set on some water to heat, and began to peel and boil the potatoes, ready for making the potato-balls.

While she was busy over this, the old man and the strange gentleman strolled out into the orchard where the old man had already dug some holes ready to plant some new young apple trees. While the gentleman strolled about, the old man went on with his work. Soon the stranger began to watch him as, holding each young tree straight, he would fill in the hole and then tramp down the earth firmly round it. Then he would drive in a good stake beside each little tree and tie the young tree firmly to it with a straw rope.

"That's hard work for an old man like you," said the strange gentleman. "Haven't you got a son who could help you?"

"Well, sir, I did have a son," answered the old man, leaning on his spade and sighing, "but he was a wild contrary lad and never much good to me! He was sharp enough, but he never cared for work and at last he ran away from home, and now his mother and I don't know what has become of him."

Presently the gentleman had another question. "Why do you tramp down the earth round the roots of each of these young trees and then tie it to one of those upright stakes?"

The old man smiled, for he thought that great folk didn't know much about tree-planting.

"Why, sir," said he, "I do all that to make the roots firm and to make the trees grow straight! Trees must be trained while they're young."

"Perhaps your son would have grown straight too," answered the stranger, "if you'd taken as much trouble rearing him as you do with your apple trees."

At that the old man only shook his head and sighed again. Neither of them spoke for a while.

"Would you know your son if he should ever come back?" asked the stranger after a time.

"Ah," said the old man, "it's true enough that he'll have changed a good bit! For, of course, he was only a bit of a lad when he ran off, but even if he has changed, we should be bound to know him, for he has a little mark on his shoulder that looks just like a bean."

"Come into the kitchen a minute," said the stranger, and then pulling off his coat and opening his shirt, he asked:

"Was the mark something like this?"

You can guess how astonished and delighted the old couple were to find that they had got their lost son back again and to find that he had become a grand gentleman. But they were not quite so delighted when he told them how it was that he had come to look like a lord and to be riding in a carriage drawn by four fine horses.

"When I left home," said he, "I fell in with a company of thieves and robbers, and soon I managed to do some work that surprised them."

"What was that?" asked his mother.

"I managed to steal an ox as it was being driven to market, and then the next day, and the next, to steal two more oxen from the very same man and then to let him have his beasts again, and all without his ever finding out who had tricked him! I ended up by stealing all the robbers' horses – stealing them clean away from the thieves who thought they were teaching me! So after that, I knew I had learned my trade and so I set up on my own as a Master-Thief. Those robbers never dared do a thing to me, or to try to get their own back. They knew I could beat them at their own trade. So now I'm rich, and there are no locks or bolts that can keep me out. I just take anything I've a mind to. But don't be afraid! I never interfere with the likes of you! I only steal from rich people who have so much money they don't know what to do with it. Poor honest people haven't anything to fear!"

His father didn't like all this at all and he shook his head.

"No good ever came of such doings!" said the old man. But his wife said:

"Thief or no thief, he's still my son!" and when the Master-Thief had kissed his mother and given her a good hug, they all sat down to their dinner of potato-balls.

And now for a while they lived peaceably, with the Master-Thief sometimes lending a hand with the work and sometimes driving about in his fine carriage.

Now, not far from the cottage, in a very grand house, there lived a rich nobleman, a Count, who had so much money that he couldn't tell how much he had got. He had also got an only daughter and a smart and pretty girl she was. On one of the days when he happened to be dressed in his smart clothes and was out driving in his grand carriage with the four black horses, the Master-Thief caught sight of the girl. He got out of the carriage very politely and went over to speak to her and there he stood with his hat in his hand, while they had a few words together. The end of that was that they liked each other very well. He indeed liked the Count's daughter so well that he soon determined that, somehow or other, he would have her for his wife. So, the very next day, the Master-Thief said to his father:

"I'd like you, if you please, Dad, to step up to the Great House this morning."

"What for?" asked his father.

"I just want you to ask the Count if I can marry his daughter," answered his son.

"You're out of your senses!" answered the old man.

"Nothing ventured, nothing have!" said the Master-Thief.

"You can't be right in the head if you can talk such silly nonsense!" answered his father. "You just keep clear of the Count, or he's sure to find out all about the life you've led and then it would be his job to get you hanged for a thief!"

"I don't mind what he knows! You can be quite honest about it, Dad!" answered his son, laughing. "Just tell the Count straight out what my trade is! But be sure to say that I'm not an ordinary thief, but a Master-Thief."

Well, you can guess that the poor father didn't at all want to go up to the Great House on an errand like that! However, his son gave him no peace, so in the end, go he did. But when, at last, he actually stood before the Count, the poor old fellow was trembling and almost sobbing with fright.

"What's the matter with you, my man?" asked the Count.

At first the old man couldn't answer, but at last he told the Count the whole story – how his runaway son had come back looking like a grand gentleman, how he said he was a Master-Thief, and how he now wanted to marry the Count's daughter.

But instead of being angry the Count only burst out laughing, and even patted the poor fellow on the back.

"Don't worry!" said the Count. "We'll soon get the better of his impudence! Don't forget that if a man calls himself Master of any trade, he has got to show a Master-Piece – a really good job – for all the world to see! We'll make your young rascal show us three Master-Pieces – just because of his impudence! Never fear! I'll make them so hard that he'll never dare call himself a Master-Thief again! Just you send him along to me."

Well, though he had heard the whole story, all the same the Count was rather surprised when a carriage with four black horses came up to the great house the next day and when such a grand and well-spoken young gentleman got out of it.

"So I hear that you fairly frightened your poor old father and that you told him that you're a Master-Thief?" said the Count.

At that the young man bowed politely.

"And what's more, I hear that you want to marry my daughter?"

The young man bowed again.

"I suppose you're willing to show me what you can do?" asked the Count.

"It will be a pleasure!" answered the Master-Thief.

"Well," said the Count, looking very sly, "just because of your impudence we'll see if you can do three Master-Pieces."

"If it's thieving, Sir Count, I shall be delighted! Just say what they are!" answered the Master-Thief.

"First," said the Count, "you must try to steal my favorite mare from the stable."

"Certainly."

"But mind, I shall have a right to have her well guarded!"

"Oh, of course!" answered the young man. "Guard her as much as you like!"

"Then, on Sunday morning, you must steal the joint that will be roasting for our Sunday dinner out of the kitchen under my very nose, and just when the cooks are busy basting it."

"That won't be too hard," answered the Master-Thief.

"And last of all," went on the Count, looking slyer than ever, "on Monday night you must steal the sheet off my bed and the nightgown that my wife will be wearing."

"As you wish, Sir Count."

"But don't forget," added the Count, "that if you can't do these three things, it's my business to

catch thieves and, what's more, to hang them!"

"Never mind about that,"

answered the Master-Thief pleasantly. "But will you, on your side, promise that if I really can do all that, you'll let me marry your daughter – and no more questions asked?"

"Yes! On the word of a Count!" and with that they both laughed. The Count laughed because he was quite sure that nobody in the world would be able to trick him three times over. The Master-Thief laughed because he enjoyed doing that sort of thing and because he felt sure that he would be able to do all that and because the prize was a pretty wife who fancied him already.

So now, when they had taken leave of each other, they each began to make their preparations for the first trial. The Count arranged that six of his grooms should watch the mare in turns day and night, three by three. The first groom was to hold the mare's bridle, the second was to hold her tail, and the third was to sit on her back.

After he had warned the grooms, and seen them all in their places, the Count went off well pleased, quite sure that, even this first time, he had set the Master-Thief an impossible task. Indeed he believed that the impudent young fellow wouldn't even try, but would drive away in his grand carriage, and take his boasting tongue far away and so, like that, he would trouble them no more.

Meanwhile the Master-Thief really did drive off in his grand carriage! But he only went to the nearest town and, when he got there, he just did a little shopping. First he bought some second-hand clothes from an old peasant woman, then he got some brown stain, then he bought a nice little barrel, then some wine to put in it, and last of all he went to an old man in a by-street who sold all kinds of drugs and medicines, and giving him rather a strange prescription, he asked him to make up half a pint of the mixture.

"Half a pint?" said the old man, when he had read the prescription. "It's powerful stuff, you know!"

"Yes, I know!" answered the Master-Thief.

Now, although it was coming on

to springtime, the nights were still cold, with a near frost, and when it got dark the three grooms (who had nothing to do except hold on to the Count's favorite mare in a draughty stable) soon began to feel shivery. It got colder and colder and quieter and quieter. Presently one of them heard someone coughing outside.

"Who's there?" called out one of them.

"Only a poor old peddler-woman!" answered a shrill voice from the darkness.

The groom who was supposed to be holding the mare's tail took one of the lanterns and went out to have a look. Sure enough, there sat an old woman all crumpled up. She seemed to have been carrying a heavy load on her back, for there it was beside her, and she was coughing and shivering pitifully in the darkness and cold.

"That's all it is," said the groom when he came back to the others. "Just an old peddler-woman! She says she's got no bed for the night and asked me could she come in and lie down on the straw. It's just starting to sleet outside! It's no night for a Christian to be out!"

The end of it was they let the old woman come in, and so in she hobbled, and she seemed so bad with her cough that one of the grooms had to help her with her burden. He noticed that the load seemed to be a small wine cask.

"What have you got in your cask, old lady?" one of them asked when they'd had a good look at it in the light of the lanterns. But she seemed to be so deaf that they had to ask her again.

"A nice mouthful of wine," said the old woman at last, between coughs. "I get a living by peddling the stuff."

"A little of that would soon warm us up," said the groom who was sitting on the mare's back to the others. Then he said:

"What would you take in exchange for a glassful?"

"Money and good words," said the old woman.

So then he felt in his pocket and the other two grooms did the same, and, after a little bargaining, each of them bought a glassful. The wine was strong and soon began to warm them.

"When wine is good, I like a second glass!" said the groom who was holding on to the bridle.

"This wine really is old, I swear! It's as old as the old woman who sells it," agreed the one who was upon the mare, and he reached down his glass for another fill, while the one who held the mare's tail soon put out his glass too. So it went on, and it wasn't long before

one groom decided that he could hold the mare's tail
every bit as well if he was sitting down, or even lying
down, while, as the bridle reins were long, the other
groom too had the same idea. So, as you can guess,
these two were soon fast asleep and snoring. And now,
somehow or other, the old woman seemed to have
stopped coughing and to be much more active than
before. Instead of hobbling she began to move about
quickly and busily, but keeping in the shadows.
Gently she loosed the hands that were still holding the
mare's tail and gently she put into their grasp a wisp of
straw instead, while the hands that had been holding
the reins soon had a piece of loose rope in them.

But now, what about the groom who still sat on the
mare's back? Peering up into his face the old woman
could see that he had noticed nothing because he was
sleeping as he sat. Nimbly the old dame unbuckled the
saddle girths, threw a couple of ropes over a beam that
was just above the mare's stall, tied the end of the ropes
to the saddle, and, pulling hard on the free ends, hoisted
the groom up, saddle and all, and made the ropes fast

to the posts of the stall. Who would have thought, half an hour earlier, that such a poor old woman with such a bad cough would have had the strength to do all that!

And now it was that the Master-Thief (for as you have already guessed, I'm sure, the old woman was none other) tucked up his petticoats, muffled the mare's feet by tying them up in old rags and, jumping nimbly on her back, rode her softly out of the stable. Out across the yard they went, and then, when they were well clear, he galloped her home to his father's stable.

It was when dawn was just breaking and when the Count was just getting up, and as he stood yawning and stretching as he looked out of his bedroom window, that the Master-Thief rode up on the stolen mare.

"Good Morning, Sir Count!" called out the rider cheerfully. "Here's your mare! Do go and look in the stable and see how comfortable your grooms are!"

Well, it was a lovely morning, the mare seemed none the worse, and the Master-Thief looked so cheerful that, though at first he felt vexed, the Count couldn't help bursting out laughing. Presently, when he came down and took over his mare again, he even clapped the Master-Thief on the back. But all the same, as he did so, he said to him:

"Don't make too sure, you young rascal, that you can just go on playing me tricks! No! Not even once more, let alone twice! Remember, tomorrow is Sunday! The Sunday one is going to be harder! However, you needn't try if you don't want to! You've still got time to use that fine carriage of yours."

"Thank you very much for the warning, Sir Count," said the Master-Thief and, this time, he pretended to look rather thoughtful, for, you see, he wanted the Count to think that perhaps he didn't mean to try the next thing, but would go off to where he came from.

As soon as he was out of sight and hearing, however, the Master-Thief began to whistle a cheerful tune. Off he walked to the village as fast as he could. There he managed to borrow a couple of hunting dogs, a net, and a sack, and then, with dogs, net and sack, he set off to the nearby mountain. By nightfall he had caught three hares, and had got them, all three safe and lively, in his sack. Then, once more whistling cheerfully, he returned the dogs and the net and went home with the three hares, very well pleased with himself, and had a good night's sleep.

Now, as the Count had reminded him, the next morning was Sunday. But though he meant to go to the Great House, the Master-Thief didn't put on his Sunday best. Not at all! He collected the oldest rags he could find and, where buttons were missing, he fastened these bits of clothes with odds and ends of string until he looked so poor and filthy that it made one's heart bleed to see him. Then, with his sack on his back, he stole into the passage at the back-door of the Count's house, just like any other beggar. The Count himself and all his household were in the kitchen, watching the roast. Just as they were most busy, the Master-Thief let one of the hares out of the sack, and it set off tearing round and round the yard in front of the kitchen's windows.

"Oh, just look at that hare!" said the folks in the kitchen, and several of them were all for running out to catch it. Yes, the Count too saw it running.

"Oh, let it run," said he. "There's no use in thinking to catch a hare in the spring!"

It wasn't long before the hare found a way to get out and disappeared.

A while afterward, the Master-Thief let the second hare go, and again they saw it from the kitchen. They all thought it must be the same hare that they had seen before, and now more of them wanted to run out and catch a March Hare, but at last this hare also managed to find a way out.

It was not long before the Master-Thief let the third hare go, and this one too set off and began to run round and round the kitchen-yard, exactly as the others had done before it. And still they all thought it must be the same hare that kept on running about, and everyone of them was eager to be out after it.

"Well, it's certainly a fine hare!" agreed the Count at last. "And it doesn't seem to know how to get out either. All right, let's see if we can't get it!"

So out he ran, and the rest with him – away they all went, the hare

before, and they after; so it was rare fun to see. But the Master-Thief didn't waste time watching. Indeed, he snatched up the roast and ran off with it; and where the Count got a roast for dinner that day I don't know; but one thing I do know, and that is, that he didn't manage to get

a hare to roast, though he ran after it till he was both warm and weary. That was twice he had been tricked!

So now, if the Count kept his word, there was only one more Master-Piece of thieving that had to be done before there could be a wedding. This was Monday's task, and what the Master-Thief had to do was to steal the sheet off the Count's own bed, and the nightgown that the Countess his wife would be wearing.

As they had done before, the Count and the Master-Thief each began their preparations. The Master-Thief waited till it was dark; then he went to the gallows; there he found a poor dead prisoner hanging. He carried the body on his back to the Great House and hid it among the trees in the garden. After that he went and fetched a ladder which would be long enough to reach up to the Count's bedroom window. As for the Count, what he did was to get a musket, load it, lay it by his bedside and go to sleep.

Presently, when the moon was up, the Master-Thief got his ladder, set it up very quietly, and then with the dead man on his back, he climbed up it. He climbed just high enough for the head of the dead man to show at the window. Then he made a bit of a noise, and he kept bobbing it up and down so that it looked for all the world like someone peeping in. The Count woke up.

"There's the Master-Thief," whispered he to his wife, giving her a

nudge. "Now you watch me shoot him," and with that he took up the musket.

"Oh, don't shoot him after telling him he might come and try," whispered his wife.

"I'll shoot him all right!" replied the Count, and he took good aim. Next time the head popped up – *bang!* The Count had shot the body of the dead hanged prisoner right through the head.

The Master-Thief, who of course had kept well out of musket shot, immediately let the body go. Down it fell, down to the foot of the ladder, landing with a thump. As quietly and quickly as the wind, the Master-Thief ran down the ladder and hid among the bushes, while the Count, getting quickly out of bed, leaned out of the window. Sure enough, there was a dead body lying on the ground.

Then the Count began to scratch his head.

"It is quite true," said he to his wife, "that I am the chief magistrate in these parts and that the Master-Thief had done plenty of crimes. But people are fond of talking and maybe they'll wonder why we didn't have a trial and all that. I believe the best thing will be for me just to go down and bury him quietly. So don't you say a word about it!"

"You must do as you think best, dear," answered his wife.

So now, down the ladder went the Count. He shouldered the body of the poor prisoner, and, taking a spade, he went off to a secret place in the garden.

No sooner had he gone and had begun to dig a grave, than the Master-Thief said to himself:

"Now's the time!" Up the ladder he climbed and in through the window and was soon in the bedroom. It was much darker in there than out in the moonlight.

"Why, dear, back already?" said the Countess, seeing a man standing there and thinking that it was her husband.

"Why yes," said the Master-Thief, in a very good imitation of the Count's voice. "I just put him into a hole and threw a little earth over him. But just let me have the sheet to wipe myself with – he was all covered with blood and I have made myself in such a mess with him!"

So that is how the Master-Thief got the sheet!

Then he went to the darkest corner of the room, and pretended to be busy with it. After a while he said:

"Do you know, I am afraid you will have to let me have your nightgown too. I'm in such a mess! The sheet won't get it all off!" So the Countess took off her nightgown and gave it to him. But now the Master-Thief had to think of an excuse to get away.

"Do you know, dear wife," said he, "I believe I must have left one of his feet sticking out! That will never do! To make my mind easy I'll go down and make sure before I go back to bed again," and then off he went down the ladder and with him he took both the sheet and the nightgown.

He was only just in time, for now the real Count had finished burying the poor prisoner. Up the ladder he came and into the room.

"Had you really left one of his feet sticking out?" asked the Countess. "And what have you done with the sheet and with my nightgown?"

"What's that?" called out the Count.

"Why, dear! I'm only asking you what you've done with the sheet and with my nightgown! You used them to wipe off the blood," said she.

Well, though they talked till it was morning, neither of them could make out what it was that had happened.

However, once daylight came, they had not much longer to wait, for they were hardly up and dressed when there before them stood the Master-Thief, and what is more, there stood their pretty daughter with him.

Well, as you know, the Count and Countess were the sort that can take a joke, and though the Countess felt a bit nervous as to what sort of husband her daughter was going to have, they had to agree to the marriage, for the Count had given his word. So now the two young people knelt before them and got their blessing. To tell the truth, the Count wouldn't have dared refuse him now, for he was almost afraid that his new son-in-law would steal everything that he had, daughter included, if he did anything to vex him.

And that was how it was that the Master-Thief became the son-in-

law to a Count, and how he became
a rich man, and how he got a pretty
wife who loved him. I don't know
whether he ever stole any more, but
I am sure, if he did, it was just for a
bit of fun and that he gave back
whatever he stole.

A German tale

Johnny-Cake

ONCE UPON A TIME an old man and an old woman lived in a little house. One morning the old woman got up and she made a Johnny-Cake (that's a cake of cornmeal bread). She put it in the pan and she put the pan on the fire. Then she said to the old man:

"I'm going out to milk the cow. Turn the Johnny-Cake as soon as it's done on one side."

Now the old man was lazy, so, instead of getting up, he lay in bed, and by and by he said to himself:

"Oh, dear, I suppose I shall soon have to get up and turn that Johnny-Cake."

"I can turn myself!" called out a voice from the fireplace.

The old man was so surprised that, at first, he couldn't move, not even when he saw the Johnny-Cake

jump out of the pan. Then, when he *did* get out of bed, the Johnny-Cake was too quick for him and, in a moment, it was through the door, and out down the garden path, rolling and hopping end over end. The old man shouted and hollered like mad:

"Stop, you Johnny-Cake! Stop, you Johnny-Cake!" and he shouted so much that the old woman stopped milking the cow and ran to see what was the matter. When she saw what was going on, she put down the milk pail and ran after the Johnny-Cake. But, run as they would, they couldn't catch him! That Johnny-Cake outran them both.

By and by they were so out of breath that they had to sit down and rest, with Johnny-Cake far away down the road.

On ran Johnny-Cake, and by and by he came to two well diggers, and when they saw what it was coming down the road they looked up from their work and they called out:

"Where are you going, Johnny-Cake?"

Johnny-Cake shouted back:

"I've outrun an old man and an old woman, and I can outrun you too-o-o!"

"Oh, you can, can you? We'll see about that!" said they, and they threw down their picks and shovels and ran after him. But it was no use, they couldn't catch up with him and soon they too had to sit down by the roadside to rest.

On ran Johnny-Cake, and by and by he came to two ditchdiggers who were at their work.

"Where are you going, Johnny-Cake?" they called out, and as he ran by Johnny-Cake shouted back:

"I've outrun and old man and an old woman, and two well diggers, and I can outrun you too-o-o!"

"Oh, you can, can you? We'll see about that!" cried the ditchdiggers, and, throwing down their spades, they ran after him. But Johnny-Cake outstripped them, and, seeing they could never catch him, they gave up the chase and sat down to rest.

On went Johnny-Cake, and by and by he came to a bear. The bear said:

"Where are you going, Johnny-Cake?"

He said:

"I've outrun an old man and an old woman, and two well diggers, and two ditchdiggers, and I can outrun you too-o-o!"

"Oh, you can, can you?" growled the bear. "We'll see about that!" and the bear got up and lumbered along as fast as his legs could carry him after Johnny-Cake, who never even stopped to look behind him.

Before long the bear was left so far behind that he saw he might as well give up the hunt first as last, so he stretched himself out by the roadside to rest.

On went Johnny-Cake, and by and by he came to a wolf. The wolf called out:

"Where are you going, Johnny-Cake?"

Johnny-Cake shouted back:

"I've outrun an old man and an old woman, and two well diggers, and two ditchdiggers, and a bear, and I can outrun you to-o-o!"

"Oh, you can, can you?" snarled the wolf. "We'll see about that!" and he set off at a gallop after Johnny-Cake. But Johnny-Cake went on and on, so fast that the wolf saw there was no hope of catching him, and lay down to rest.

On went Johnny-Cake, and by and by he came to a fox that lay quietly in a corner of the fence. The fox called out to him in a sharp voice, but without getting up:

"Where are you going, Johnny-Cake?"

Johnny-Cake shouted back:

"I've outrun an old man and an old woman, and two well diggers, and two ditchdiggers, and a bear, and a wolf, and I can outrun you too-o-o!"

"I can't quite hear you, Johnny-Cake," said the fox softly. "Won't you come just a *leetle* closer?" and with that the fox pricked his ears and turned his head to one side.

Then for the first time Johnny-Cake stopped his race, and he did go a little closer, and he called out in a very loud voice:

"I'VE OUTRUN AN OLD MAN AND AN OLD WOMAN, AND TWO WELL DIGGERS, AND TWO DITCH-DIGGERS, AND A BEAR, AND A WOLF, AND I CAN OUTRUN YOU TOO-O-O!"

"I still can't quite hear you, Johnny-Cake! Won't you come a *leetle* closer?" said the fox in a weak voice, and as he spoke he stretched out his neck toward Johnny-Cake, and put one paw behind his ear.

Johnny-Cake came up quite close this time, and leaning toward the fox, he screamed out louder than before:

"I'VE OUTRUN AN OLD MAN AND AN OLD WOMAN, AND TWO WELL DIGGERS, AND TWO DITCHDIGGERS, AND A BEAR AND A WOLF AND I CAN OUTRUN YOU TOO-O-O!"

"Oh, you can, can you?" yelped the fox, and with that he snapped up Mr. Johnny-Cake in the twinkling of an eye.

Although this version comes from America, its origin is British. There is also a Scottish version called The Wee Bannock.

If you are reading this story aloud, chant the chorus (Johnny-Cake's answers) and try to give the impression that it is being loudly and tauntingly called back to the listener by the rapidly vanishing Johnny-Cake. Make the final "too-o-o" very loud. And, at the climax, when the sly fox grabs the unsuspecting Johnny-Cake, spring at your listeners and scream "OH!" to make them all jump.

My Berries

Here is my tale.
Let it come from me to you.

LONG AGO in Africa, not in my village, there lived a boy. His name was Ucaijana. That means Little Weasel. He got his name because he always thought he knew better than anyone else!

He was so cheeky that he thought nothing of going out to the cattle kraal – the paddock and the cattle shed – and then sitting down among the grown-up men and eating beef with them. My children, you will agree, this was very shocking! A boy ought not to do it!

In the boys' hut, he made a nuisance of himself as well, for he was always boasting, pretending to be grown up and not doing his share of the work that all the boys were supposed to do.

So the other boys got sick and tired of Little Weasel.

"Go away," they said, "and never come back!"

"Very well," said Little Weasel, "I shall go. I don't want to stay with you! I shall manage better all by myself!" So he set off down the path – out and away – into the bush.

He hadn't gone far when he met a big bird – Crane – stalking along on his thin legs.

"Mr. Crane," said Little Weasel, "I know where to find nice juicy berries! Come with me, I'll show you." Crane agreed and Little Weasel showed him. They both ate as many berries as they wanted and then Little Weasel suggested that tall Crane with his long beak should pick the berries that grew up high. So Crane did this and they hid them in a hole – to eat next time they were hungry.

Then Mr. Crane and the boy said good-bye. Crane, that big, serious bird, went stalking off by one path, and Little Weasel went scampering off by another. By and by Little Weasel sat down to rest.

And then, oh my children, he began to feel hungry again. So what did he do? I'm sorry to tell you that he went back and, all alone, Little Weasel ate up the store of berries! He didn't leave one!

Then he began to shout:

"Crane! Mr. Crane! Come quick! Come quick!" Crane heard and came walking back along the path on his long legs.

"Mr. Crane! Some thief has eaten all the berries! It must have been *you*! You're the only one who knew where they were hidden!"

"No, Little Weasel, it wasn't me!" said Mr. Crane in his deep bass voice.

"It's very unfair," said Little Weasel. "I ought to be paid for the berries, *my* berries, that you've eaten!"

Then Little Weasel sat down on the ground with

his arms folded over his head and rocked himself
backward and forward as if he was crying, and he
began to sing – over and over again:

"My berries! My sorrow! My berries!"

"Oh, dear," said Mr. Crane, "I really don't know *what* can have
happened! But I'll tell you what I'll *do*, you poor little fellow! I'll give
you one of my feathers!"

With that, he pulled out one of his best, longest, and most beautiful
white feathers and gave it to Little Weasel. Little Weasel stopped crying
and took the feather, and set off on his journey again.

He hadn't gone far when he came to a place where a crowd of young
warriors were dancing a war dance and throwing spears and assegais.
Little Weasel sat down to watch.

"Here's a fine feather for one of you to wear!" called out Little Weasel.

One of the handsome young warriors took the feather and stuck it in
his hair! But after a while, as he whirled and twirled, dancing, the wind
blew the feather away.

"Your feather's lost! Now what's to be done, Little Weasel?" said
one of the dancers.

"Never mind," said Little Weasel. "You can pay
me if you can't find it again."

So they all went on dancing.

At last the sun began to go down and then
one of the handsome young warriors remembered
Little Weasel.

"Hello, you funny little fellow! Has anyone given
you back your feather?"

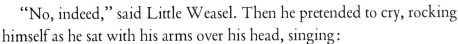

"No, indeed," said Little Weasel. Then he pretended to cry, rocking himself as he sat with his arms over his head, singing:

> *"Alas, my big feather!*
> *That I got from my brother the Crane,*
> *The Crane that ate the berries.*
> *My berries! Oh, my sorrow! My berries!"*

The warriors said, "We really must give this poor little fellow something." But what? They couldn't give him an assegai, no! Not a war assegai, because you see he was only a boy. So they gave him a nice fish spear.

Next day, Little Weasel came to a river. A lot of people were fishing, but all they had got were bits of sharp maize-stalk and sharpened bits of bamboo. But these are *not* as good as a proper fish spear!

"Ho!" called out Little Weasel. "Use my fish spear! You can borrow it in turns."

So one of the men took it and now he was able to spear much better. Fish after fish! Everybody was dancing about and shouting, they were so pleased!

At last, one man took careful aim and he hit a very big fish. Such a fish!

But, oh my children, the spear was stuck in the fish and now fish and spear are disappearing into the water! Just imagine! They're going down, down, to the very bottom of the deep dark river!

"Oh, Little Weasel," they said, "your spear's gone!"

"Well, let it go! You can give me the worth of it!" said Little Weasel.

All day Little Weasel had been sitting there, but now the sun began to go down and everybody began to get ready to go home. They had forgotten!

"I want the worth of my fish spear, please!" said Little Weasel at last. Nobody took any notice. Then he sat down just as before and began to sing:

> *"Alas, my fish spear, that I got from*
> *the young warriors playing at war.*
> *The young warriors playing at war*
> *that lost my big feather,*
> *The big feather that I got from*
> *my brother the Crane.*
> *The Crane that ate all the berries,*
> *My berries!*
> *Oh, my sorrow! My berries!"*

The people listened. "Well," they said, "it certainly does seem rather hard that this poor little fellow shouldn't have the value of his spear." So they tied up a bundle of the fish. They tied it up nicely in wet grass and gave it to Little Weasel.

It was evening by now, and soon he came to a village. All the people were having supper. They just had maize porridge. They hadn't got anything to eat with it.

"Porridge without any relish!" said Little Weasel. "Have some fish!" While they were cooking the fish, Little Weasel went to sleep and when he woke up those people had finished – porridge, fish and all!

"What?" said Little Weasel. "You've eaten everything?"

"Yes, we have!"

Then he began to sing:

> *"Alas, my fish that you have eaten,*
> *The fish that I got from the people*
> *fishing with maize-stalks,*
> *From the fisherman that lost my fish spear.*
> *The fish spear that I got from*
> *the young warriors playing at war.*
> *The young warriors that lost my feather,*
> *The feather that I got from*
> *my brother the Crane.*
> *The Crane that ate the berries,*
> *My berries that I found!*
> *Oh, my sorrow! My berries!"*

"Well," they said, "we've eaten all the fish so we can't give it back, but here is some maize to make porridge," and they gave him a big bundle of maize cobs.

Next day, Little Weasel came to some people who were sitting by the path having a meal, and they had nothing to eat but sour milk.

"What?" said Little Weasel. "Is sour milk all you've got? You'd better grind this maize and cook it with the milk."

So they ground the maize between two stones and cooked it and they gave some – not very much – to Little Weasel, and they ate it with the sour milk.

Presently, Little Weasel said it was time for him to go on with his journey and would they please give him the value of the maize.

"What?" they said. "We thought it was a present!"

"But it was a great *big* bag!" said Little Weasel.

Then he sat down on the ground with his arms over his head and this is what he sang:

> "Alas, my maize corn that you have eaten,
> The maize that I got from people
> who were eating porridge without any relish.
> The people who ate my fish,
> The fish that I got from people
> fishing with maize-corn stalks,
> From the fisherman who lost my spear.
> The fish spear that I got from
> the young warriors playing at war.
> The young warriors that lost my feather,
> My big feather that I got from
> my brother the Crane.
> The Crane that ate my berries,
> My berries that I found!
> Oh, my sorrow! My berries!"

"Well," they said, "we can't give you back the maize corn, that's certain! But perhaps *this* will do?"

So they gave him a fine big milking bowl, and Little Weasel went on with his journey.

After a time he came to where some herd-boys were milking their cows, but all they had to milk the cows in were bits of broken crock. They hadn't got proper bowls, not even gourds, so, as you can guess, a lot of the milk was spilled.

"Here! You take this. You'll manage a lot better!" said Little Weasel.

Well, they did. In turn the herd-boys used his bowl, no milk was spilled and each boy drank from the lovely bowl. Once, twice, they filled it and drank.

But what do you think happened? They were going to fill it a third time, but one of the cows kicked it with her hind foot and broke it to bits.

Little Weasel sat on the ground and cried. He began rocking himself with his arms over his head, and this is what he sang:

"Oh, my milking-bowl that I got from
the people with nothing for supper but sour milk.
The people that ate all my maize,
The maize that I got from people
who were eating porridge without any relish.
The people who ate my fish,
The fish that I got from people,
fishing with maize-corn stalks,

From the fisherman that lost my fish spear.
The fish spear that I got from
the young warriors playing at war.
The young warriors that lost my feather,
My big feather that I got from
my brother the Crane.
The Crane that ate my berries,
My berries that I found!
Oh, my sorrow! My berries!"

When they heard this sad song, the herd-boys didn't know what to do! They really felt quite sad, but then one of them remembered that once, long ago, they had found a real war assegai hidden in the bush – a splendid one, so splendid that only a chief ought to carry it.

So, as they were only boys and couldn't use it, they had hidden it again. But because Little Weasel belonged to another tribe, it might be all right for him to have it.

So one of them ran to fetch it and they gave it to Little Weasel.

"There," they said. "That's in return for your big bowl that the cow kicked to bits!"

Little Weasel was so pleased that he didn't know what to say, but just rushed away with the splendid war assegai.

What do you think he did then, oh my children?

Instead of going on with his journey, he turned back and went home again as fast as he could.

When he came to the village all the men stared at him.

"Little Weasel! Oh, Little Weasel! Where did you get that splendid war assegai? Don't you know, you rascal, that that's the kind that only chiefs can carry?"

"Of course I know!" said Little Weasel in a very grown-up voice. "Didn't *you* know? I AM a chief now!"

Some of them only laughed.

"I wonder!" they said.

"You don't know much," said Little Weasel. Then some of them began to think. Could Little Weasel be telling the truth for once?

"As he's got such a splendid war assegai, he *might* have become a chief!" one of them said in a doubtful voice.

"Of course I have," said Little Weasel.

In the end, half the people in the village agreed that as he'd been clever enough to get himself such a splendid war assegai, Little Weasel really must be a chief.

But the others said, "No! It is all nonsense!"

They couldn't agree, so half the people went off with Little Weasel as their chief, and made a new village.

This is my story! Now tell me yours.

Little Weasel is an African example of a folk-hero found in stories all over the world — one who is impish and slightly fraudulent. If you enjoyed this story, you may also enjoy the New Zealand story of Maui — a trickster and a boaster — who, nonetheless, fished the two New Zealand islands out of the sea.

Baba Yaga

FAR, FAR AWAY in Russia, very long ago, there lived a couple who had one daughter. They lived in a log hut on the edge of a huge forest. She was a beauty, that girl; Marusia the Fair they called her. Her skin was as white as milk, her lips as red as blood, and the hair on her head black and glossy as a crow's wing. And what's more, Marusia was as kind and good-natured as she was pretty.

After a while her mother died. Then what did Marusia's father do,

but marry again. A bad woman she was, the one that
he married, and she soon grew to hate Marusia.

One day, while the man was out working, the stepmother said
to Marusia:

"I want to make a new spring dress for you, my dear, so you must go
and borrow needles and thread from my sister who lives in the forest."

Well, the girl was willing, but she had to ask her stepmother which
paths she should take. As soon as her stepmother began to tell her, poor

Marusia grew pale, for what her stepmother was telling her sounded just like the way to Baba Yaga's hut.

Now, as Marusia well knew, this Baba Yaga was the worst witch in all Russia. She had iron teeth, her legs were nothing but bare bones, and she rode through the air in a mortar which she drove along with the pestle. She lived in a very queer kind of hut too, for it stood on chicken's legs and whichever way you tried to come up to it, the hut would turn round and stare at you with its windows.

What was poor Marusia to do? Her father was working far away and she did not dare to disobey her stepmother. So she tried to be brave. After all, there might be a real aunt who lived in the forest, and if so, she would have been frightened about nothing. So, thinking she might have a long walk, Marusia packed up some food in a red handkerchief, and set off.

She walked and she walked through the thick, dark, beautiful forest, and then, much sooner than she had expected, she came to a clearing and there she saw a hut.

But what sort of a hut? You may well ask. The hut stood on chicken's legs just as she had feared, and it seemed to Marusia that, as she came toward it, it turned round to stare at her with its windows. Poor Marusia! However, it did no good to feel frightened, for she was quite sure that the hut had seen her. So she tried to open the rickety gate in the fence.

"Ooh! Augh!" squeaked the gate. It sounded just as if opening hurt its hinges. Without thinking what she was doing, Marusia felt in her pocket, and there at the very bottom was a little bottle of oil. She poured some oil into each hinge and went through the gate.

As soon as she got into the yard she saw that a girl was standing there.

She didn't look much older that Marusia. She was crying bitterly, and when Marusia asked her who she was, she said that she was Baba Yaga's servant and that the old witch had just pinched her black-and-blue in one of her wicked tempers. As she was crying and telling Marusia all this, she was all the time trying to push the loose hair out of her eyes.

Without thinking what she was doing, Marusia untied her little bundle, put what was left of the food she had brought in her apron pocket and gave the nice red handkerchief to the poor little servant girl to tie round her head to keep the hair out of her eyes. The poor child was so surprised at getting a present and kind words, that she couldn't say thank you, but only made a little bob-curtsey and smiled.

On went Marusia, and just as she got to the door of the hut, a miserable, thin dog bounced out at her from a kennel and began to bark his head off. Without thinking what she was doing, Marusia fished in her pocket and pulled out a piece of bread. She gave it to the dog, who ate it as if he hadn't had anything to eat for days.

And now at last, Marusia had to knock at the door of the hut.

"Come in," answered a grating voice.

Marusia opened the door and there sure enough, she saw old Baba Yaga herself, iron teeth, bone legs and all. She was sitting at a loom, weaving. As she wove, the loom made a noise: *Ter clack! Ter clack!*

"Good morning, Auntie," says Marusia in her sweet voice.

"Good morning, my dear," says horrid old Bony-Legs.

"Stepmother has sent me to ask you for the loan of needles and thread to sew me a dress."

"I'll see what I can find," says the witch with a grin. "Sit down at the loom and weave a little, while I go and look."

So the witch stood up and Marusia sat down. She began to work the loom – *Ter clack! Ter clack!* – and then Baba Yaga hobbled outside on her bony legs. Baba Yaga wasn't thinking about needles and thread. Oh no! Marusia soon knew that, when she heard what she said to the servant girl:

"Go and get sticks, light a fire, and heat the bath. Draw plenty of water and scrub my niece. Scrub her nice and clean. I'm going to eat her."

But the servant girl didn't want to heat the bath and she didn't want Marusia to be eaten, for Marusia had spoken kindly to her and given her a red handkerchief. Though she was afraid of the witch, she walked slowly, and as for getting on with making a good fire, she fetched only one stick at a time. And as for the bath water, well, she fetched that in a sieve.

But Baba Yaga didn't notice this. She had begun to walk round the hut so as to listen and make sure that Marusia hadn't run away. "Are you weaving, little Niece?" she called out.

"Yes, Auntie, I'm weaving." And weave she did, so that the loom went *Ter clack! Ter clack!*

Presently Marusia looked up from her work and saw that a thin cat was sitting in the corner of the hut. Without thinking what she was doing, Marusia put one hand into her pocket and picked out a little bit of bacon. She threw it over to the thin cat, which ate it up in a twinkling. Then as the cat stretched her paws and began to lick herself, saying to Marusia:

"Little girl, if you take my advice, you'll try to get out of here."

Just then Baba Yaga passed by the window.

"Are you weaving, little Niece?"

"Yes, Auntie, I'm weaving," answered Marusia again, and *Ter clack! Ter clack!* went the loom.

They listened for a moment till Baba Yaga had gone on.

"Here's a comb for you and a towel," went on the cat softly. "They aren't what you think. Try to get away, and if Baba Yaga chases you, throw the towel behind you. If she chases you again, throw down the comb."

"Thank you, Cat," said Marusia. "But how can I get out of here? If I stop weaving, she'll soon miss the *Ter clack! Ter clack!* She'll know that the loom has stopped."

"I'll see to that," answered the cat. "Let me come where you are."

So Marusia stood up and the cat sat down. *Ter clack! Ter clack! Ter clack!* went the loom. If that thin cat wasn't much good at weaving, it was a grand one for muddling everything about. You can hardly imagine the mess it made with Baba Yaga's threads. Warp and woof! Woof and warp! All tangled and crossed up. The worse the muddle got the more the cat smiled. As for Marusia, she slipped quickly out through the door at the other side of the hut and went through the gate.

Baba Yaga came back, and again she listened below the window.

"Are you weaving, little Niece?"

"Yes, Auntie, I'm weaving," answered the thin cat in a squeaky voice, trying to mimic Marusia. As it spoke its claws were tangling every thread on the loom worse than ever.

Soon Baba Yaga came back into the hut. What was her fury when she saw that there was no Marusia weaving at the loom, only the thin

cat making a dreadful mess.

"How dare you play me such a trick?" shouted Baba Yaga to the cat in a rage.

"Long as I've served you," hissed the cat, "you've never given me so much as a bone. But Marusia gave me bacon."

Baba Yaga rushed out of the hut. There was the thin dog.

"Dog, why did you let her escape?" shouted the witch. "You should have barked and flown at her throat!"

"Long as I've served you," growled the dog, "you've never given me anything better than burnt black crust. But Marusia gave me a thin slice of white bread the very first time she saw me."

Baba Yaga rushed on and first she shouted at the servant girl and then at the squeaky gate. But the servant girl said to her:

"Long as I've served you, you've never given me so much as a rag, but Marusia gave me a red handkerchief the first time that she ever saw me."

"Long as I've served you," said the gate, "you've never done anything to cure my pitiful creaks and groans. But Marusia oiled my hinges the very first time she heard them."

When she got such answers Baba Yaga flew into a worse rage than ever. She gnashed her iron teeth, jumped into her mortar and gave a terrific push with the pestle. Away she went, flying along in pursuit of Marusia. *Gnash! Gnash!* went her iron teeth, *Clatter! Clatter!* went her pestle.

But Marusia had been running as fast as she could and, by this time, she had got quite a long way down the path which led through the forest. All the time as she went she listened. Yes! Something was coming. She could hear *Gnash! Gnash! Clatter! Clatter!*

"That must be Baba Yaga," said Marusia to herself. "I'd better do as the thin cat told me." So she threw down the towel.

Almost before it touched the ground, the towel had become a wide river – a wide brimming river. And Marusia was on one side, and Baba Yaga was on the other. The magic river was so wide that the old witch couldn't possibly cross it with one push of her pestle, so she had to come down to earth. Oh, how she gnashed her iron teeth with spite!

However, Baba Yaga wasn't going to be beaten by a thin cat and a little girl. She had a big barn full of oxen. She went quickly to it and drove all the oxen down to the river. They were so thirsty that as soon as they got there they drank up every drop of water. Then Baba Yaga was able to make one hop of it, and like that she and her mortar crossed over.

All this time Marusia had gone on running and was a lot farther away, but she wasn't far enough. Baba Yaga was soon able to catch her up, so fast did she travel in her mortar. When she saw how close the witch was, Marusia remembered the thin cat again, and threw down the comb. Almost before it touched the ground, a huge new forest sprang up. The trees were much taller than the trees of the real forest – so tall and so close together that there was no way of getting through them or over them. But Baba Yaga set to work with her iron teeth and began to gnaw

at the huge trees. But it was all in vain. However hard she worked, for one tree that she gnawed down, the magic forest grew two more. When she saw that, Baba Yaga knew that she was beaten at last and went back in disgust.

Meantime, Marusia's father had come home to the hut.

"Where's Marusia?" he asked the stepmother.

"Oh, I've just sent the child to her aunt's to borrow needles and thread."

Just as she spoke, in rushed Marusia, quite out of breath with her hair flying and her clothes all torn. When she saw her father she threw herself, sobbing, into his arms.

"What's the matter with you?" asked her father.

"Oh, Father, Father," sobbed Marusia, "Stepmother sent me to Auntie's to ask for needles and thread, but it was no Auntie of mine. It was Baba Yaga. She meant to eat me."

"How's this, how's this?" said the father, looking sternly over the girl's shoulder at the stepmother.

With that Marusia told her father the whole story, about the hinges, the servant girl, the dog and the thin cat. As she told the tale, the stepmother soon began to see that it was all up, and, before Marusia had finished, she had slipped off and away into the forest.

Whether she ever got to Baba Yaga's hut, or whether she was eaten by a bear, doesn't matter either to you or to me. What is certain is that not long afterward the little servant girl, followed by the thin dog and the thin cat, came running down the forest path to Marusia's hut. Marusia and her father welcomed them and neither they, nor Marusia, nor her father, ever saw that bad stepmother or Baba Yaga again.

This is a good example of a traditional Russian story that has delighted many children. If you would like to read more Russian fairy tales try Old Peter's Russian Fairy Tales *chosen by Arthur Ransome.*

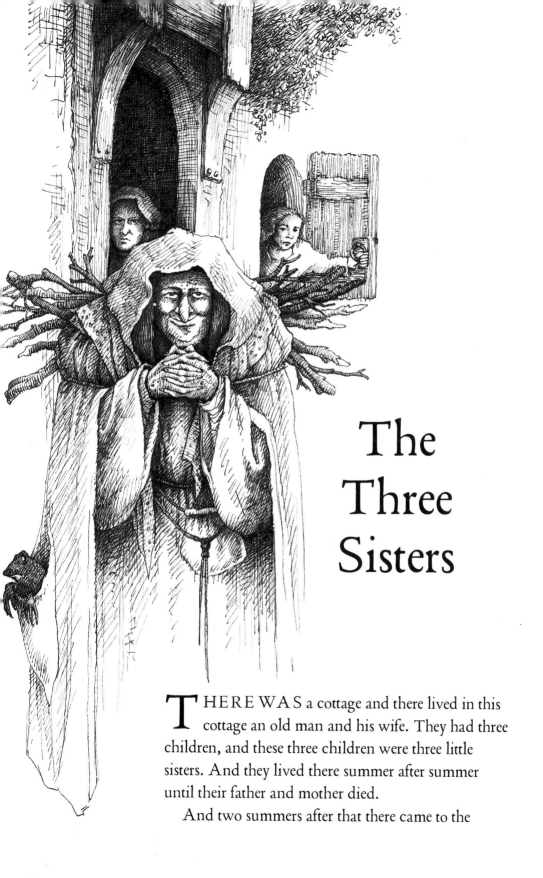

The
Three
Sisters

T HERE WAS a cottage and there lived in this
cottage an old man and his wife. They had three
children, and these three children were three little
sisters. And they lived there summer after summer
until their father and mother died.

And two summers after that there came to the

cottage a little old woman who wore a red cloak. And she went to the door and begged for a cup of tea.

"No," said the eldest sister, "we haven't enough for ourselves."

"I will bind your head and your eyes, if I don't bind your whole body," said the crone to her. With that she went away.

And now these three sisters grew poor. And one day the eldest sister said to the other two:

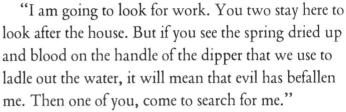

"I am going to look for work. You two stay here to look after the house. But if you see the spring dried up and blood on the handle of the dipper that we use to ladle out the water, it will mean that evil has befallen me. Then one of you, come to search for me."

And so each day in the morning, when they got up, the two sisters who stayed at home used to look for these tokens.

The eldest sister journeyed far, and farther yet, to where the devil never wound his horn and the cock never crew. Night fell. Presently she saw a little man in a red jerkin. She didn't know it, but the red-jerkined fellow was brother to the old woman of the red cloak.

And before the girl had asked him anything, he put a question to her:

"Are you looking for work?"

"Yes," said the girl.

Little Red Jerkin gave her no hint of the trials that lay before her. He opened the gate:

"Go up there, and you'll get work."

Up she climbed. There were little white stones along by the path all the way up the hill. "Stop and look!" cried one white stone.

The girl stopped and looked at the stone. She was bewitched into a trance and changed into a white stone.

That, you see, was how old Red Cloak did as she'd said. She had bound the girl's head and eyes with a spell; she had bound her whole body.

The next morning, at home at the cottage, the second sister got up and went to the door. She opened the door, and there was the spring dried up and blood on the handle of the dipper that they used to ladle out

the water. Horror came over her when she saw these things.

"Some evil has befallen our sister," she called out to the youngest girl. Then the spring flowed and the dipper was bright again.

Now she, in her turn, said to the youngest sister, "If you see the spring dried up and blood on the dipper, some misfortune has overtaken me. Come then, and look for me."

So now the second sister journeyed to where the devil never wound his horn and the cock never crew, until she, too, met this man in the red jerkin. And before she could utter a word to him, Red Jerkin spoke to her:

"Are you looking for work?" asked he.

"No," answered the girl, "I am looking for my sister."

"Your sister is up there; she has found work and is doing well."

The gate was opened and the girl climbed up the hill.

"Stop!" cried one white stone. The girl did not pause, but went straight on.

"Look!" called another pebble to her. But the girl went on.

"Look! Here is your sister!" cried a third stone.

She stood still and looked round when she heard this about her sister. And then she too was bewitched into a magic trance, and turned into a white stone.

The youngest sister was alone at home now. She got up one morning and went to the door and opened it. There was no water in the spring; it was dried up. There was blood on the dipper! Then the youngest sister burst into tears. But she had more spirit than the other two. She knew not where they had gone. She knew not where to look for them. But, after fastening the door, she took the road on which she had seen both her sisters set out.

So she too journeyed far and farther yet, to where the devil never wound his horn and the cock never crew, until she too met the little fellow in the red jerkin. Before he could open his mouth, the youngest sister spoke to him. This time it was the girl who got in first. She asked him about work.

"Yes, there is work for you." But this time Red Jerkin's heart was well-nigh broken because the maiden had got in the first word. He opened the gate and the girl climbed up the hill. As she climbed, one white stone cried out to her, "Stop!"

The girl went on.

"Look!" cried a second stone.

"This is the place!" cried a third stone.

The maiden was quite fearless. She paid no heed to them.

"Look, here are your two sisters!" cried yet another stone.

"Kiss them, then," said she, and on she went, never stopping until there were no more stones or pebbles and she reached the little old woman in the red cloak.

When Red Cloak saw the girl she fell on her knees before her.

"Have you found me then, little lady?"

"I have," said the girl (the little lady).

And now, lo and behold! All that sleepy and slumbrous spell was broken. And all those white stones and pebbles got back their former shapes. It was this maiden who had broken the whole enchantment. The girl – the little lady – wasn't afraid, and she went to her two sisters and led them up to the old woman in the red cloak.

"Here are my two sisters," said she.

"I know them," answered Red Cloak. "But it is you, my little lady, who are mistress here now. All is left in your hands. Do as you will."

"I thank you, good aunt," she answered.

Red Cloak showed the youngest sister where a great hoard of treasure was hidden. Then the girl gave her two sisters each a bagful of gold, and told them to send her word if any danger should ever befall them. And they both fell on their knees before their youngest sister. They were escorted home. And she became the greatest lady in all that land, far and wide, and she married Red Jerkin, who had become a tall, handsome young fellow. And they live there happily to this day.

A German tale

Mr. Miacca

TOMMY GRIMES was sometimes a good boy, and sometimes a bad boy, and when he was a bad boy, he was a very bad boy.

His mother used to say to him:

"Tommy, Tommy, be a good boy, and don't go out of our street, or else Mr. Miacca will get you."

But still, on the days when he was a bad boy he would go out of the street. One day, sure enough, he had scarcely got round the corner, when Mr. Miacca caught him and popped him into a bag, upside down, and took him off to his house.

When Mr. Miacca got Tommy inside the house, he pulled him out of the bag and set him down, and felt his arms and legs.

"You're rather tough," says he, "but you're all I've got for supper, and you'll not taste bad boiled.

But, body o'me, I've forgotten the herbs, and it's bitter you'll taste without herbs. Sally! Here, I say, Sally!" And he called Mrs. Miacca.

So Mrs. Miacca came out of another room and said:

"What d'ye want, my dear?"

"Oh, here's a little boy for supper," said Mr. Miacca, "but I've forgotten the herbs. Mind him, will ye, while I go for them."

"All right, my love," says Mrs. Miacca, and off he goes.

Then Tommy Grimes said to Mrs. Miacca:

"Does Mr. Miacca always have little boys for supper?"

"Mostly, my dear," said Mrs. Miacca, "if little boys are bad enough, and come his way."

"And don't you have anything else but boy-meat? No pudding?" asked Tommy.

"Ah, I loves pudding," says Mrs. Miacca, "but it's not often the likes of us gets pudding."

"Why, my mother is making a pudding this very day," said Tommy Grimes, "and I'm sure she'll give you some, if I asked her. Shall I run and get some?"

"Now, that's a thoughtful boy," said Mrs. Miacca, "only don't be long and be sure to be back in time for supper."

So off Tommy pelted, and right glad he was to get off! For many a long day he was as good as good could be, and never went round the corner out of the street.

But somehow, he couldn't always remember to be good. And one day he went round the corner again and, as luck would have it, he hadn't scarcely got round it when Mr. Miacca grabbed him up, popped him in his bag, and took him home.

When he got there, Mr. Miacca dropped him out, and when he saw who it was he said:

"Ah, you're the youngster that served me and my missus such a shabby trick, leaving us without any supper! Well, you shan't do it again. I'll watch over you myself. Here, get under the sofa, and I'll sit on it and watch the pot boil for you."

So poor Tommy Grimes had to creep under the sofa, and Mr. Miacca sat on it and waited for the pot to boil. And they waited, and they waited, but still the pot didn't boil, till at last Mr. Miacca got tired of waiting, and he said:

"Here, you under there, I'm not going to wait any longer. Put out your leg, and I'll stop you giving me the slip."

So Tommy put out a leg, and Mr. Miacca got out a chopper, and chopped it off, and popped it in the pot. Suddenly he calls out:

"Sally, my dear! Sally!" and nobody answered. So he went into the next room to look for Mrs. Miacca, and while he was there, Tommy crept out from under the sofa and ran out of the door. For you see, it wasn't his own leg, but the leg of the sofa that he had put out.

So Tommy Grimes ran home, and he never went round the corner again until he was old enough to go alone.

The means by which Tommy Grimes gets out of the clutches of a Dark Power, Mr. Miacca in this British tale, can be found in other tales too. For example, in the Grimms' Hansel and Gretel, *Hansel pokes out a stick instead of his finger.*

Mr. Miacca was not always to be feared. He not only punished bad children, but rewarded the good by leaving them presents.

133

The Laidly Worm
of Spindlestone Heugh

IN BAMBOROUGH CASTLE once lived a King who had a wife, and a son named Childe Wynd, and a fair daughter, Princess Margaret. Childe Wynd went away to seek his fortune and soon after he had gone, the good Queen died. The King mourned her long and faithfully, but one day, while he was hunting in the south country, he saw a lady of great beauty, and fell so much in love with her that he determined to marry her. So he sent word that he was going to bring a new Queen to Bamborough Castle.

Princess Margaret was not very glad to hear of her mother's place

being taken, but she did her father's
bidding and, on the day when the
new Queen was expected, she came
down to the castle gate with the keys
all ready to hand over to her
stepmother. Soon the procession
drew near, and the new Queen
came toward Princess Margaret,
who bowed low and offered her the
keys of the castle. The girl stood
there modestly with blushing cheeks
and eyes on the ground, and said:

"O welcome, Father dear, to
your halls and bowers and welcome
to you, my new Mother, for all that's
here is yours." And again she
offered the keys.

One of the knights who had
come from the south with the new
Queen, cried out in admiration:

"Surely this northern Princess is
the loveliest of her kind."

At that the new Queen flushed up and cried out:

"At least your courtesy might have excepted me!" And then she
muttered below her breath, "I'll soon put an end to her beauty."

Only a month had passed when, one night, the Queen, who was a
noted witch, stole down to a lonely dungeon which she had chosen
wherein to do her magic, and there, with spells three times three, and
with passes nine times nine, she cast Princess Margaret under her spell.
This was it:

> "I spell ye to be a Laidly Worm,
> And unspelled shall ye never be
> Until Childe Wynd, the King's own son,

The Laidly Worm of Spindlestone Heugh

*Come to the heugh and thrice kiss thee;
Until the world comes to an end,
Unspelled shall ye never be."*

So Lady Margaret went to bed a beautiful maiden but she rose up a Laidly Worm – a loathsome dragon. When her damsels came in to dress her in the morning, instead of the Princess, they found a dreadful scaly creature on the bed which uncoiled itself and came toward them. But they were afraid and ran away.

shrieking and the Laidly Worm crawled and crept, and crept and crawled, getting bigger and bigger and more and more frightful, till it reached the heugh or rock of Spindlestone. Round this it coiled itself and it lay there basking, with its terrible snout in the air.

Soon the country round about had reason to know of the Laidly Worm of Spindlestone Heugh. For hunger drove the huge creature out from a cave that it had found and it used to kill and devour everything it could come across. So at last they went to a mighty warlock and asked him what they should do. Then he consulted his great books and his familiar spirits and this is what he told them:

"The Laidly Worm is none other than the Princess Margaret, and it is hunger that drives her out to do such deeds. Put aside for her seven cows and each day, as the sun goes down, carry every drop of milk they give to the stone trough at the foot of the heugh. Then, when she has the milk to lap, the Laidly Worm will trouble the country no longer. But if this is not enough, and if she is to be unspelled so that she may have back her natural shape, and if she who put the spell and curse on her is to be rightly punished, then you must send over the seas for her brother, Childe Wynd."

All was done as the warlock advised. For a year and a day the Laidly Worm lived on the milk of the seven cows, coming down every night to lap it, so that the country was troubled no longer. But when word had been got to Childe Wynd, he swore a mighty oath that, come what might, he would rescue his sister and be revenged against the cruel stepmother.

Three and thirty of his men took the oath with him and then they set to work and built a longship with a sail and great oars. Now this was a very special ship, for they made her keel out of the wood of the rowan tree. When all was ready they out with their oars and pulled sheer for Bamborough Keep.

But as the ship came across the sea, the stepmother knew, by her magic power, that her stepson was near and that something was being done against her, so she summoned her familiar imps and gave them her orders.

"Childe Wynd," says she, "is coming over the seas, but he must never land. Raise storms, or bore a hole in the hull of his longship. Do what you will, but make certain that he does not touch shore."

So her imps went out to meet Childe Wynd's ship, but when they got near, they found they had no power over her, because her keel was made of the wood of the rowan tree. So back they came to the Witch-Queen. But now she knew not what to do, except to order her men-at-arms to try to beat back Childe Wynd and his men by force if he should try to land in any cove. Then, by a fresh and terrible spell, she caused the Laidly Worm to come down from its cave and to wait by the entrance to the harbor.

As the ship came near, the Worm was obliged by the spell to unfold its long scaly coils, to dip into the sea, and to catch hold of the longship, banging it off the shore.

Three times he tried to land, and then Childe Wynd ordered the ship to be put about and the Witch-Queen thought he had given up the attempt. But, instead of that, he only rounded the next point and landed safe and sound in Budle Creek, where the men-at-arms had not thought his ship would venture. Then, with sword drawn and bow bent, he rushed up, followed by his men, to fight the terrible Worm that had kept him from landing.

But the moment Childe Wynd had set foot on ground, the Witch-Queen's power over the Laidly Worm had gone. So, when he came rushing up, the huge thing made no attempt to hurt him but, just as he was raising his sword to slay it, the voice of his own sister came from it saying:

> "O, quit your sword, unbend your bow,
> And give me kisses three;
> For though I am a poisonous Worm
> No harm I'll do to thee."

Childe Wynd let the point of his sword fall, but he did not sheath it, for he did not know what to think and feared still that some witchery was afoot. Then said the Laidly Worm again:

> "O, quit your sword, unbend your bow,
> And give me kisses three;
> If I'm not won ere set of sun,
> Won never shall I be."

Then Childe Wynd sheathed his sword and went close to the Laidly Worm and kissed it once; but no change came over it. Then he kissed it once more; but yet no change came over it. For a third time he kissed the loathsome thing, and then, with a hiss and a roar, the Laidly Worm reared back and there, before Childe Wynd, stood his sister Margaret. He wrapped his cloak about her, and then together they went up to the castle.

When they reached the keep, Childe Wynd went to find the Witch-Queen where she sat in her bower all alone. When he saw her he touched her with a twig of the magic rowan tree. No sooner had he done this than she shriveled up, and shriveled up, till she became an ugly toad, with bold staring eyes, a scaly skin, and a horrible hiss. She croaked and she hissed, and then slowly she hopped away down the castle steps.

Then Childe Wynd took his father's place as King, and they all lived happy after.

But to this day, a loathsome toad is seem at times haunting the neighborhood of Bamborough Keep, and the wicked Witch-Queen is that Laidly Toad.

A tale from the Borders between England and Scotland

White-Faced Siminy

IN OLDEN TIMES, when a girl wanted a place as a servant, off
she would go to a hiring fair.

Well, one day, there was a young farm girl who wanted a place, so off
she went to the fair like the rest. She stood with the others and each one
had a posy of flowers to show that they were all seeking a new place.

One girl was hired and another was hired, but there she stood. At last, toward evening, a funny-looking little old man came along, hired the farm girl and off they went to his house.

He seemed a nice fellow and they had supper together. Afterward, while they were sitting beside the fire, he told her that in his house he expected the servant to call things by their proper names.

"What would you call me, for instance?" said he.

"Master, or mister, or whatever you please, sir," said she.

"No," said he, "you must call me *Don Nippery Septo*. And what would you call these?" said he pointing to his shoes.

"Slippers, or shoes, or whatever you please sir."

"You must call them *hay-down treaders*, my dear. And what would you call these?" He pointed to his trousers.

"Breeches, or bags, or whatever you please, sir."

"No, you must call them *fortune's crackers*. And what's this?" said he, pointing to the staircase.

"Steps or stairs, or whatever you please, sir."

"Not a bit of it, my girl! That's the *wooden hill* and up there is my *barnacle*," he said, pointing to where his bed was, up above. "And what would you call her, now?" asked he, as he stroked the cat.

"Cat, or Kit, or whatever you please, sir."

"No, no! You must call her *White-Faced Siminy*. And this here?" and he pointed at the fire.

"Fire, or heat, or whatever you please, sir."

"Dear me, no! It's *hot cockolorum*. And what is this?" He showed her what was in the bucket.

"Water, or wet, or whatever you please, sir."

"Not at all! That's *pondolorum*. And what would you call this?" said he, pointing to the house.

"Cottage, or house, or whatever you please, sir."

"No! No! *Great Castle of Strawbungle* is its name."

That very night, the girl, in a fright, woke up her master and this is what she said:

"DON NIPPERY SEPTO! Get out of your BARNACLE and put on your

HAY-DOWN TREADERS and your FORTUNE'S
CRACKERS. Come down the WOODEN HILL as fast
as you can, for WHITE-FACED SIMINY has got a spark
of HOT COCKOLORUM on her tail and unless we get some more
PONDOLORUM, the GREAT CASTLE OF STRAWBUNGLE will soon be
all on HOT COCKOLORUM!"

An English tale

Anansi and Mrs. Dove

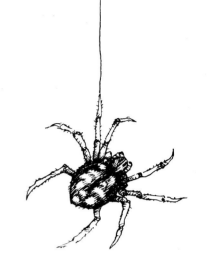

O NCE IN A LONG-BEFORE TIME,
before Queen Victoria came to reign over we,
in dis country – dat's Jamaica – dere live Anansi –
Anansi sometimes he man, sometimes he one great big
spider. But him always bad. One mornin' Anansi,
him hear somet'ing, make him very please. Him know
a long time dere was an old witch living near named
Five, and him know she not like dis
name, not at all. She want a buckra
name (dat's de sort of name de white
folk have). But all de time, all de
people still call her Five and dat
make her terrible vex. Dis morning
dis is what Anansi hear when him
was standing outside de old witch's
back yard and peeping through
small hole in de fence.

*Anansi and
Mrs. Dove*

Dis old witch she making a big Obea – dat's a big magic. She boil up herbs. Don't know what she didn't boil up as well, and now him see de pot is smoking and how she take her Obea stick and him hear how she call out terrible strong spell. She say dat anyone dat say de word Five, bound to tumble down dead, on de ground.

Anansi creep away. Him rub his hands, very pleased. Him say to himself, "Dis could be a good livin' for me and for me starvin' wife and children." Den what he do?

Him go early de next morning to where de path to de village was, along by de stream he go. All de people going to dat village bound to come dat way when dey go to de market to buy red peas and white peas and akees (dat's a lovely fruit dat grow in Jamaica) and all sort of nice t'ings. When Anansi get to dis place by de path, him make five heaps right near by de path. Den him sit down, wait.

By and by Mrs. Duck came along de path (Quack, quack, quack), going to de market.

"Good mornin', Mrs. Duck," says Anansi.

"Good mornin', Anansi," says Mrs. Duck. "Quack, quack, quack."

"Me hopes you is quite well?"

"T'anks, Anansi, quack, quack, quack, me is quite well."

"Oh, Mrs. Duck," says Anansi, looking sorrowful, "me is such a silly fellow. Me want to grow few yams" (dat's like sweet potatoes) "and me make me yam heaps all right like you can see. But now me can't count dem, Please, kind Mrs. Duck, will you count me yam heaps for me?"

"Certainly, Anansi. Quack, quack, quack. Me will count you yam heaps for you."

Den what Mrs. Duck do? She begin to count.

"One, two, t'ree, four, five," and de minute she say "Five" she tumble down dead on de ground, and den dat bad Anansi eat her all up. Him never save not one bit for his starvin' wife and family. When Anansi finish de last scrap, his very happy. Den him sit down and wait some more.

After a while along come Mrs. Rabbit (Hip hop), flappin' she's long ears and nibblin' de green grass.

"Good mornin', Mrs. Rabbit. Me hope you is quite well?"

"T'anks, Anansi, me is quite well." She mouth full wid grass when she speak so it sound funny.

"Oh, Mrs. Rabbit," says Anansi, "kind Mrs. Rabbit, me is such a silly fellow. Me make nice yam heaps here by de path. But now me can't count dem. Please Mrs. Rabbit, will you count me yam heaps for me?"

"Certainly, Anansi," says Mrs. Rabbit, and she wave she long ears most polite. Den she begin to count.

"One, two, t'ree, four, five," and de minute she say "Five", Mrs. Rabbit she tumble down dead on de ground.

You think Anansi save one bit

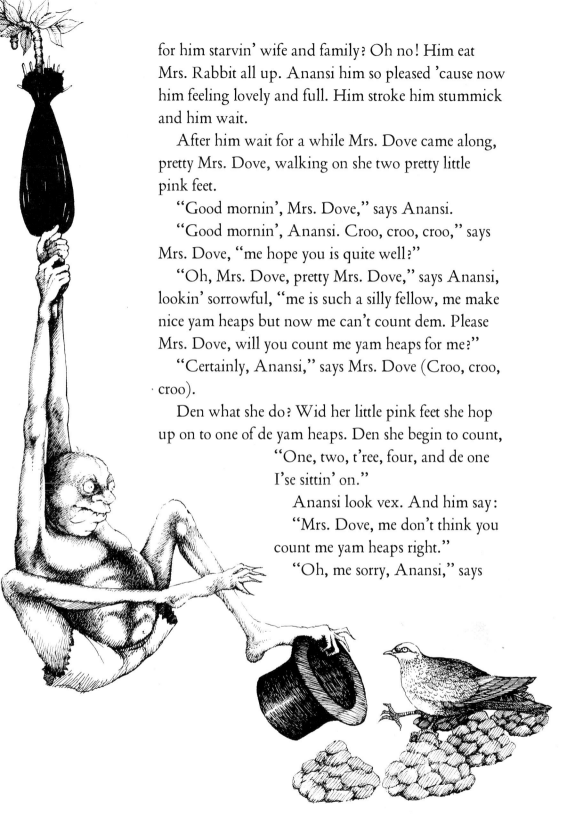

for him starvin' wife and family? Oh no! Him eat
Mrs. Rabbit all up. Anansi him so pleased 'cause now
him feeling lovely and full. Him stroke him stummick
and him wait.

After him wait for a while Mrs. Dove came along,
pretty Mrs. Dove, walking on she two pretty little
pink feet.

"Good mornin', Mrs. Dove," says Anansi.

"Good mornin', Anansi. Croo, croo, croo," says
Mrs. Dove, "me hope you is quite well?"

"Oh, Mrs. Dove, pretty Mrs. Dove," says Anansi,
lookin' sorrowful, "me is such a silly fellow, me make
nice yam heaps but now me can't count dem. Please
Mrs. Dove, will you count me yam heaps for me?"

"Certainly, Anansi," says Mrs. Dove (Croo, croo,
croo).

Den what she do? Wid her little pink feet she hop
up on to one of de yam heaps. Den she begin to count,

"One, two, t'ree, four, and de one
I'se sittin' on."

Anansi look vex. And him say:

"Mrs. Dove, me don't think you
count me yam heaps right."

"Oh, me sorry, Anansi," says

Mrs. Dove (Croo, croo, croo). "Me count dem again for you." Den she count dem again, "One, two, t'ree, four, and de one I'se sittin' on."

"Dat not right," says Anansi. "Me SURE dat not right."

"Me so sorry, Anansi," say sweet, pretty Mrs. Dove (Croo, croo, croo). "Me try again," an' she count again. "One, two, t'ree, four and de one I'se sittin' on."

Anansi very vexed. Him so furious him forget all about what de witch say and he bawl out:

"You silly Mrs. Dove! You stupid Mrs. Dove! One, two, t'ree, four, FIVE!" and when him say "FIVE", Anansi tumble down dead on de ground.

Mrs. Dove she shake she feathers an' she hop down from de yam heap an' she go off to the market quite cool an' pleasant to buy red peas, an' white peas, an' akees, an' all sort of nice t'ings.

This Anansi story was told to Amabel Williams-Ellis while she was in the West Indies — with "incredible verve"!

The Folk Lore Society has published a collection of Anansi stories — and the music that goes with them.

Tamlane

LONG, LONG AGO, Fair Janet lived in her father's castle. He was the Earl of March and a great lord.

In the castle tower, she and the other damsels sat sewing their silken seams, but Fair Janet kept looking up from her sewing, out of the window. She saw the trees of Carterhaugh Forest where the damsels had been forbidden to go, as this was where the young knights of Elfland came to hunt and play. It was said that harm would come to any maid that went there.

However, one day, she could bear it no more. She let her sewing fall

from her lap and silently slipped off to the greenwood. Just inside the forest she saw a fine horse tied to a tree. It was as white as milk and it had golden trappings. She went on to the next glade and was plucking a rose growing there when a handsome young man called out:

"How dare you pluck that rose, Fair Janet, and come to Carterhaugh Forest without my leave!"

"I shall pluck a rose whenever I please," she said, tossing her head, "and I shall never ask leave of you!"

At her bold answer the young knight spoke her fair and laughed,

shaking the nine silver bells that
hung at his girdle. Then all day
Janet and young Tamlane danced
in the forest and it seemed as if sweet voices sang among the trees:

"Fair and fair and twice as fair
And fair as any may be,
Thy love is fair for thee alone
And for no other lady.

My love is fair, my love is gay,
As fresh as are the flowers in May."

When the sun went down, Fair Janet knew she must hurry home before
she was missed. She looked so wan and pale that the ladies playing in the
castle asked what she had seen. The next day Fair Janet sat drooping and
sad. She longed to be back in the greenwood with young Tamlane,
singing and dancing. An old gray knight said to her, "Alas, I think it's
with the fairies you've been, Fair Janet. If your father hears of this we
shall all be blamed, for no good ever came of going with the fairies."

"Hold your tongue, old knight," she wept. "Oh, if my love were an
earthly knight he would be the finest bridegroom that any maid might wed.

The steed on which my true love rides
Is fleeter than the wind;
With silver he is shod before,
With burning gold behind."

Although Janet spoke boldly, she feared in her heart that the old man

was right and that Tamlane might
be an elf knight. When she could
bear it no longer, she again slipped
off to the greenwood. As Tamlane appeared she said,
"Tell me. Are you a christened soul, or, as I fear, an elf knight?"

Tamlane told her that though he lived at the Elf Queen's court he was
christened, the son of a knight and a lady:

> "Roxburgh he was my grandfather,
> Took me with him to bide;
> And once it fell upon a day
> As hunting I did ride,
> There came a wind out of the north,
> A cold wind and a snell,
> A dead sleep it came over me,
> And from my horse I fell;
> And the Queen o' Fairies she took me
> In yon green hill to dwell."

He said Elfland was a fair country and he would live there for ever
but for one thing.

"What is that one thing?"
Janet asked.

He told her that every seven years,
the Queen of Elfland must pay a
ransom to the foul fiends and he
feared that this time she meant to
pay with him, unless someone could
break the spell and win him back
from her. Then Fair Janet asked
how this might be done. He said
that there was no time to lose as on
Halloween, the very next night, the
fairies rode abroad. Any damsel

who would win back her true love
from them must keep vigil at Miles
Cross for him.

Janet said, "How shall I know you in the gloom of
night? Surely you will be with a pack of knights the like I never saw."

Tamlane replied, "You must go to Miles Cross in the deep of the
night and fill a cup with holy water, then make a circle round you with
it. The fairies will ride past in companies. Let the first company ride past
and say nothing. Let the second company pass likewise, but I shall be
riding with the third company.

> *O first let pass the black, lady,*
> *And then let pass the brown;*
> *But quickly run to the milk-white steed,*
> *And pull his rider down.*
>
> *For some ride on the black, lady,*
> *And some ride on the brown;*
> *But I ride on the milk-white steed,*
> *A gold star on my crown:*
> *Because I was an earthly knight*
> *They give me that renown.*
>
> *My right hand will be gloved, lady,*
> *My left hand will be bare,*
> *And that's the tokens I give thee,*
> *No doubt I will be there.*

When you know me, you must take my horse by the bridle and snatch the reins from me. When you let them fall, I shall slip down from my horse and the Queen will cry out, 'True Tamlane's stolen away.' Then come fair, come foul, you must hold me tightly. First they will turn me to a newt, then to a snake, then to a wild deer. Hold it fast. I will then be turned into a bar of red-hot iron, but if you love me you must not let go, however much it burns.

> *They'll shape me in your arms, Janet,*
> *A mother-naked man;*
> *Cast your green mantle over me,*
> *And so shall I be won."*

Tamlane then vanished. At sunset the next day, Janet stole away to the greenwood and in the deep of the night went to Miles Cross. She made the circle of holy water around her and she waited.

> *About the dead hour of the night,*
> *She heard the bridles ring;*
> *And Janet was as glad of that,*
> *As any earthly thing.*

Everything happened just as Tamlane had told her. First a company of knights rode by on black horses, and then a company on brown. But when at the head of the third company she saw the milk-white steed, she rushed forward, seized the bridle, and down slipped the rider. There rose an unearthly cry: "True Tamlane's stolen away."

And now, instead of holding her true love in her arms, Janet found that she was holding a great newt, then a snake, and then a wild deer. Still she gripped tightly. Then in her hands she found a red-hot iron bar. But burn as it would, she held, knowing that this was the only way to have her heart's desire.

> *They shaped him in her arms at last,*

A mother-naked man;
She cast her mantle over him,
And so her love she won.

Then up and spake the Queen of Fairies
Out of a bush of broom;
"She that has borrowed young Tamlane
Has gotten fair bridegroom."

Out then spake the Queen of Fairies,
And an angry woman was she,
"She's taken away the bonniest knight
In all my companies!"

"Farewell to you, Tamlane," the Elf Queen cried.
"But know you this. If I had known yesterday what I
know tonight, I would have changed your heart of
flesh for one of stone, your two gray eyes to eyes of
wood, and I would have paid a ransom seven times to
the fiends so that I could have kept you."

Then she and her knights vanished and Fair Janet
and Tamlane went back to the castle where they were
married amidst great rejoicing.

An English tale

The Waterfall

ONCE UPON A TIME there was no water anywhere near a certain tall mountain in China and, except for what they could save when it rained, people had to walk a great distance to carry all their water from a little stream. Water was as precious as could be.

In a village near Tall Mountain, there lived a girl with sleek, black hair, so long that it fell almost down to her ankles. She used to wear it coiled up on her head and on her neck. People called her Sister Long-Hair.

Sister Long-Hair lived with her mother who was paralyzed and bed-ridden. And the girl kept pigs to keep them in food. Every day, after coiling up her hair, she would go to the little stream, a great distance away, to fetch water for the pigs and for themselves. Then she would

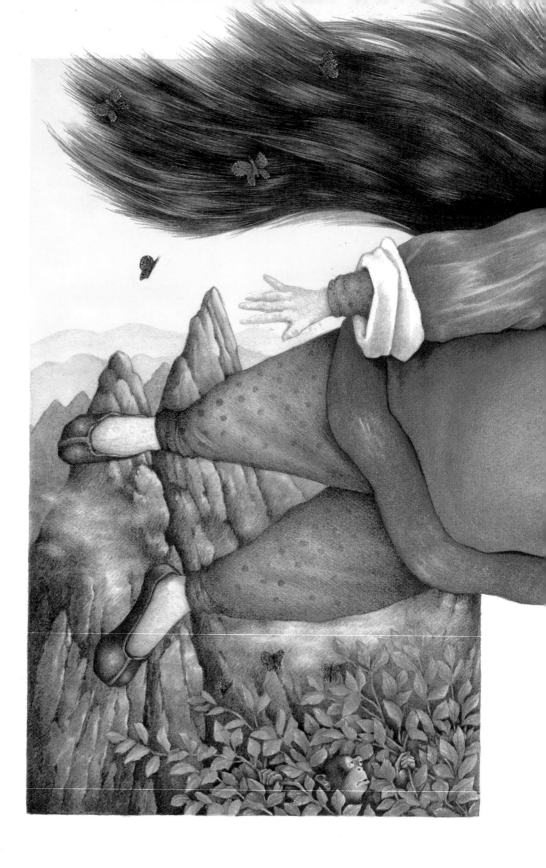

climb up the tall mountain to collect grass for fodder. She was busy from morning till night, what with that and looking after her poor, sick mother.

When she went up the mountain to fetch the grass she always rested by a tall banyan tree. She always felt that tree was very friendly. She liked sitting there, and sometimes she thought it hummed a little tune to her.

One day, after she had been resting under the banyan tree as usual, she climbed farther up the mountain and scrambled across a big chasm to a place she'd never been to before. And there, what should she see, but a beautiful turnip growing out of a rock. Its green leaves glistened like emeralds. Well, she thought that it would make a nice meal. She grasped the leaves, gave a tug, and up came a round root, quite a big one, the size of a teacup. It left a hole in the rock, and from this hole, clear water slowly began to trickle. But when it had trickled a little, the turnip flew out of her hand and landed with a plop back in the hole, and the water stopped coming.

Now the girl was thirsty, so she pulled up the turnip again and waited for the water and then drank. The water tasted cool and sweet, as sweet as pear juice. When she had finished drinking, the turnip flew out of her hand once more and replanted itself in the hole, and the water stopped flowing. The girl stood up and stared, but suddenly a gust of wind carried her across the chasm into a cave. There, sitting on a rock, was a strange-looking man whose body was covered with yellow hair.

She heard him say in a voice of fury:

"I am the mountain god. You've discovered the secret of my mountain spring. If you let a single person know what you've found or if anyone else comes near here to get water, I shall kill you." And with that, a second gust of wind carried the girl even farther. It carried her right back to the foot of the mountain.

As she walked home she began to think. She wanted badly to tell her mother and the villagers about the mountain spring, but she was afraid. Every time she thought about that hairy man, she shuddered.

Sister Long-Hair had always been a happy girl, but now she was changed. She became slow and dull. She looked at the cracked earth and the wilted crops, for there was a bad drought at that time. She watched the men and women, old and young, go every day to scoop up water from that little stream a great distance away. They sweated and they strained. And yet she kept thinking all you had to do was to pull up the turnip and chop it in pieces so that it couldn't pop back again, then make the hole bigger. Surely then water would flow down the mountain?

She opened her mouth to say, "On Tall Mountain there is . . ."; then she thought of the yellow, hairy man and swallowed the words.

She couldn't eat and she couldn't sleep for longing to tell the secret. Her long hair was no longer sleek and black, but dry and brittle. Her mother said, "Child, what ails you?" People in the village touched her brittle hair, and they too asked, "Child, what ails you?" but the girl bit her lips and stayed silent.

Days went by and the days grew into months. She worried so that her long hair turned from black to snow white. She couldn't be bothered to comb it or coil it up. She just let the long tresses hang round her.

She leaned against the gate before her house and watched the people pass. She kept murmuring to herself, "On Tall Mountain there is . . ."; then she stopped.

But one day she saw an old, white-bearded man walking unsteadily with a pail of water at either end of his carrying pole, and he slipped on a stone and fell, the water spilled and his pails were broken. He'd injured his legs and blood ran from the cuts. She hurried to help him. She tore a piece of cloth from her dress to bind up his legs. The old man moaned and his face twisted in pain.

She murmured to herself, "You, my girl, are afraid of death. Just because you're afraid of death the earth is cracked and the crops withered. Everyone sweats and strains and the old man has injured his legs." She beat her head with her hands. At last she could bear it no longer. Suddenly she shouted to the old man:

"Grandpapa, there's a spring on Tall Mountain. Just pull up the turnip, chop it in bits, then make the hole bigger and spring water will gush down the mountain. It's true, it's true, it's true, I saw it with my own eyes."

Without waiting for the old man to answer, she jumped to her feet and with her long white hair flying she ran through the village shouting:

"There's a spring of water on Tall Mountain. Just pull up the turnip and chop it in bits, then make the hole bigger and spring water will gush down the mountain. It's true, it's true, I saw it with my own eyes."

Then she told the people how she had found the spring, but she

didn't say anything about the old
man in the cave, the mountain god.
The villagers always thought she
was a good-hearted girl, so they believed what she said and a whole lot of
them, carrying choppers and picks, followed her up Tall Mountain and
across the chasm.

And there, sure enough, were the beautiful bright-green leaves of the
turnip. It was the girl herself who pulled the turnip up with both hands
and she flung it down on the rocks.

"Chop it up quick! Chop it up quick, everyone!" The choppers
came down and chopped the turnip up into bits, and water welled up
from the rock hole. But the hole was only as big as a teacup and flowed
very slowly.

"Open it up with your picks, everyone. Make an opening as big as
you can. Hurry, hurry!" she cried.

The picks went to work, and the hole quickly became as big as a rice
bowl, then it grew to the size of a pail, then it grew to the size of an
earthen water-crock. Clear water flowed down the mountain. And all
the people from the village who had come up the mountain laughed and
shouted with joy.

Just then, there came a great gust of wind which carried off the girl.
The villagers were so happy watching the water that they didn't notice

that she'd disappeared until
somebody said, "Where's Sister
Long-Hair?"

"Oh, I expect she went home to
tell her mother the good news,"
another one said. Then they
scrambled down the precipice and came back down
the mountain and back to the village.

But she hadn't gone to the village, as you can guess.
She'd been snatched away by the mountain god. In
his cave he scolded her and roared at her:

"I told you not to tell anyone, and yet you've
brought all these people up here to chop up my turnip
and hack open the rock hole. Now I'm going to
kill you."

"I'm ready to die," she said coolly.

"I'm not going to let you die easily," said the
mountain god, grinding his teeth. "I'm going to make
you lie on the precipice so that the spring water will
dash against your body from above and you'll suffer for
a long, long time."

"For the sake of getting that water to the village, I
am willing to suffer," she said calmly. "I've only got
one request. Let me go home first to get someone to
take care of my poor old mother and the pigs."

Well, the mountain god wasn't sure that he would,

but at last he said, "All right, but if you don't come back, I'll tell you what I'll do. I'll seal up the mouth of the spring and I'll kill everyone in the village, including your mother, so that it will be worse than if you hadn't interfered. And when you come back, don't disturb me any more. I don't ever want to see you again. Just go and lie on the edge of the precipice down which the waterfall falls, and be sure you *don't disturb me any more!*"

The girl nodded and a gust of wind carried her to the foot of the mountain just as it had the first time. She looked at the spring water tumbling down the mountain, she looked at the water flowing into the fields, and in her imagination she could already see how, later on, the crops would grow green. She laughed with happiness.

When she got home, she didn't dare tell her mother the truth, so she said:

"Mother, water is flowing down from Tall Mountain. We shan't have to worry about water any more, and now the girls in the next village have invited me to visit them for a few days. I'll ask Auntie from next door to come and look after you and the pigs."

When she'd arranged this she came back and, brushing her mother's cheek, she said:

"Mother, I might stay more than a few days, I might stay more than ten days in the next village."

"Yes, of course, my dear," said her mother. "I shall be well looked after. Don't hurry. You deserve a rest. Stay longer if you like."

With tears in her eyes the girl kissed her mother and then turned to the door.

"Mother, I'm going," she said, and she walked toward Tall Mountain
with her white hair flowing behind her.

Now, she thought to herself that she'd have a rest, as she generally did, by the shady banyan tree where she'd so often rested. She patted the tree trunk, saying, "Oh, great and kind banyan tree, I shall never come to rest under your shade any more." As she spoke a tall old man walked out from behind the tree trunk. He had green hair and a green beard and he was wearing green robes.

"Where are you going, little maiden?" he asked.

She sighed but didn't answer.

"You needn't answer," the old man said. "You're a good girl and I want to save you, so I've done something that may succeed. I've chiseled a figure out of stone to look just like you. Come behind the tree and have a look."

The girl walked round the tree and, sure enough, there was a stone statue very much like herself, except for one thing — it had no hair, no hair at all.

"I know that the mountain god wants you to lie on the edge of the precipice and be pounded to death by the water, but I'm going to carry this stone girl up the mountain and put her to lie where you should lie. But the only thing that it needs is your white hair. What are we going to do?"

He looked at her and after a few minutes went on:

"Sister Long-Hair, are you willing to bear pain, and let me pull out your hair so that it can be given to the stone girl? If you do that maybe the mountain god won't suspect that it's only a stone image and not you."

Well, anyone who's ever had their hair pulled out in handfuls knows how *that* can hurt, but she nodded her head and the old man began to pull out her hair, hair by hair, and lock by lock. When he'd finished he put the hair on the head of the stone girl and, strangely enough, it immediately stuck.

"Go home, girl," he said to her. "The fields will

have water now. Go and cultivate them with the others. Life in your village will get better and better." Then in a moment – he must have been very strong – he picked up the stone girl and ran up Tall Mountain. She watched and she saw how the green man set the stone girl down on the edge of the precipice and let the water dash against it, and the white hair hung over the precipice and the water flowed down it – water like white hair!

The girl leaned against the banyan tree and stared. Suddenly she felt her head itching and rubbed it. Ah! There was something there!

Her hair was growing again! And in five minutes it hung almost to the ground just as it had before. She looked again. It was sleek and black, sleek and black. She stayed a long time under the banyan tree, but the old green man didn't come back. Suddenly a gentle breeze rustled the banyan leaves and a voice said:

"Sister! Sister Long-Hair! The mountain god has not woken up. He never guessed. You can go home now."

A Chinese tale

The Fifty Red Night-Caps

ONCE UPON A TIME, there was a man who had fifty red night-caps to sell at a fair. His wife put them into a great bag for him which he carried over his shoulder.

Now it was a very hot country and presently the man's way lay through a wood. When he came to the

shade, he put down his bag and sat down to rest, and soon he took one of the red night-caps out of his bag, put it on, lay down and went to sleep.

Now there were monkeys in that wood, and by and by, a great old monkey came stealing down out of the trees, seized one of the red night-caps out of the bag, popped it on his head, and ran up into a tree and sat there grinning and chattering. By and by, another monkey came stealing down and he too took a red night-cap, put it on and ran up into a tree and he too sat in the tree grinning and chattering. And then another monkey took another red night-cap, and then another, until at last there were forty-nine monkeys in forty-nine red night-caps, sitting in the trees chattering and calling out to each other.

At last they all made such a noise that the man woke, and when he was awake, and saw nothing but the empty sack in front of him, he cried out:

"Oh, what shall I do? What shall I say to my wife when I take back neither the red night-caps nor the money I was to get for them?"

In his despair he seized his red night-cap off his head and threw it on to the ground.

Whereupon the forty-nine monkeys seized their forty-nine red night-caps and they also threw them down to the ground. Whereupon the man picked up all the night-caps, put them back into the bag, threw the bag over his shoulder, and went off and sold them at the fair.

The Bear in
the Coach

I T WAS A VERY COLD NIGHT, and it was very dark
in the coach. When the traveler got in he saw that there was only
one other passenger. Nothing was said for a long time. At last the
traveler said:

"It's a very cold night, sir."

"Grr . . ." said the other passenger.

"That is a beautiful fur coat you are wearing, sir."

"Grr . . ." said the other passenger.

"Would you allow me to stroke it?" said the traveler.

"Grrr . . ."

"Guard! Guard! There's a bear in the coach! There's a bear in the coach!"

But the bear let down the window, jumped through it, escaped over the country, and was never seen again.

These two stories, The Bear in the Coach *and* The Fifty Red Night-Caps, *were told by Amabel Williams-Ellis's grandmother to her mother; by her mother to herself; and by Amabel Williams-Ellis to her own children and grandchildren.*

The Great
Greedy
Beast

Long, Long ago
there were some people who
lived in a nice valley among the
mountains; this was in Africa. The
only way to get to the village where
they lived was through a narrow
place – what they called a *nek*. The
mountains round about were so
high and steep that you couldn't get
in to the valley any other way and
the *nek* really was very narrow.

One day a Great Greedy Beast
was feeling very hungry. He crawled
and he crawled until he came to the

nek and he put his nose down and he snuffed, and he could smell people and cattle, and hens, and all sorts of live things.

Well, he hadn't had any food for quite a long time, and he was hungry and he wasn't fat any more, wasn't that Great Greedy Beast. He tried to follow that delicious smell and he tried to get through the narrow *nek* in the mountains. For a long time he couldn't, but at last he got so thin that he just managed to squeeze through. Then the dreadful creature ate everything he could find in that village!

He ate all the people, did that Great Greedy Beast. He ate all the dogs, all the cows and all the hens. At least he *thought* he had eaten every living thing and everybody!

But there was a woman with a new baby who had seen him coming – just this one woman – and he hadn't smelled her. This was because as soon as she spied him she had smeared herself all over with the ashes from the dust heap and she had smeared her baby all over with the same dust. Then she had gone out of her hut where she lived, and she had crept into a little hut where they generally kept the calves.

When the Great Greedy Beast had finished eating all the people and all the cattle and all the goats, and all the dogs and all the hens, he went round to see if he had left anything. He put his snout close to the little hut where the woman and her baby were hiding and he snuffed! And then he snuffed again! But all he could smell was gone-away calves and ashes, so he too went away.

Away he crawled. He crawled and he crawled till he came to the *nek* in the mountains.

He had once been thin and hungry, but now this Great Greedy Beast had eaten such a lot that he was fat and all swelled out. He was so fat now that try as he would, he couldn't get through and so, of course, he had to stay where he was.

That Great Greedy Beast didn't bother about this. He thought that not being able to get out didn't matter that much! He felt sure that he had eaten everything there was to eat, so there was no one left to attack him, so he could just lie there and go to sleep. So that was what he did. He just shut his eyes and slept.

But as soon as the Great Greedy Beast had crawled out of the village and off to the *nek*, the woman opened the door of the little hut. Then she dusted off the ashes she had rubbed on herself and she dusted her baby as well. All those ashes had made her thirsty and she thought she had better go and get some water. Also she wanted to make sure that the Great Greedy Beast hadn't drunk all the water in the river, as well as eating all the people and animals. So she set down her baby in the hut and off she went down to the river and had a drink.

But when she came back, instead of her baby, she found a grown man – a splendid warrior – sitting there in the little hut that was used for calves.

He was a splendid man, this warrior, armed with spears and bush knives and with a huge shield.

"Man!" said she in fright. "What have you done with my baby?"

"Mother," said he in his deep man's voice, "I *am* your baby."

"But you were only born the day before yesterday!" said she.

"Never mind about that," said he. "What has happened? Where have all the people gone?"

At this his mother began to sob. "Oh," said she, "the people have all been eaten by the Great Greedy Beast, as well as all the cattle, the dogs, the sheep and the goats and the hens."

"That must be a terrible sort of monster!" said he.

"Yes, he is that!" said she, "but I managed to hide you from him all the same."

"Well, where is the Great Greedy Beast?"

"Come out and let us see, my child," said she.

So the woman and the splendid warrior with his spears and his leopard-skin belt with his big knives with antelope-horn handles stuck in it, climbed on to the roof of the calves' hut. Then his mother pointed up to the *nek*, which was the only way of getting to their valley, and she said:

"Son, do you see that thing with a head that nearly fills up the *nek*? Well, that thing really isn't part of the mountain, *that* is the Great Greedy Beast!"

"Well," said he, "we'll soon see to that!" And he began to climb down off the roof of the hut.

He had three spears with him and a shield and these big knives as well. Off he strode! And his mother followed him, and called out to him:

"But, son, you were only born the day before yesterday! You're not going to try and fight that terrible monster?"

"Oh yes, I am," said he, "you'll see, Mother dear. It'll be all right!"

Well, as you can guess, his mother couldn't stop him! So off he went. He walked with long strides to the *nek* where the monster lay. But he stopped twice on the way.

Why? To sharpen his spears and his knives on flat stones. When he got near, the monster smelled him, and when it smelled him it opened one eye and then it opened its huge mouth to try to swallow him.

But you see, it was stuck! It couldn't turn! It had eaten so much that
it couldn't get up, so when it opened that huge mouth the warrior just
skipped aside and got behind the monster's jaws. Then, with all his
might, he stabbed it once, twice and thrice, in the back of the neck, once

with each of his three spears, and at
the third spear stab, it died.

Next the warrior took one of the
big knives with antelope-horn handles that he had in
his belt and he began to cut. Soon, from inside the
animal, a man's voice said, "Oh, don't cut me!
Don't cut me!"

So he left off cutting in that place and began to cut
again, lower down. But now came another voice from
inside and this one said "Moo-moo." (That, as you
can guess, was one of the cows that the Great Greedy
Beast had swallowed.) Once more the warrior stopped
cutting and began at a third place.

This time, from inside the Great Greedy Beast, he
heard a different sound, a "Kwee! Kwee! Kwee!"
(That was a shrill dog's bark, as you can guess.)

So for a fourth time he began
cutting at yet another new place.
"Cock-o-cock-a-loo!
Cock-o-cock-a-loo!" (You can
guess what that was.)

But this time the warrior shouted:
"I'm sick and tired of cutting in
new places! You're only a cock, just
you get out of the way yourself!" So
the cock moved over and the
warrior went on cutting and he cut
until he opened a big door in the
side of the Great Greedy Beast.

Then, when it was open, all the people and the children and the sheep, goats, cattle and all the dogs and cats and chickens came out, all of them alive and well!

The end of it was that they made the warrior a chief and they made his mother a chieftainess, and all the people and the children feasted and danced and drummed and shouted for joy because their new chief and chieftainess had saved them all from the Great Greedy Beast.

There is usually something remarkable in all traditions about the birth or childhood of a folk hero. Like Hercules, this "splendid warrior" wastes no time on being an infant.

This African tale has other links with Asian and European folk stories – as with Jonah and the Whale, and the Grimms' Seven Little Kids there is an unexpected, happy, ending – that of getting out alive and well from the insides of a predator.

Tom-Tit-Tot

ONCE UPON A TIME there was a woman who baked five pies, but when they came out of the oven, they were dreadful. Slow-baked they were, so that the crust was too hard to bite. She said to her daughter:

"Daughter," says she, "you put those there pies on the larder shelf and leave 'em there a little and they'll come again." (She meant, you know, that the crust would get soft.)

But the girl was too greedy.

"If they'll come again," says she to herself, "I may as well eat 'em!" Then would you believe it, the girl set to work and she ate them all – first and last!

Supper time came and the woman, who'd been hard at work at her spinning, felt hungry and she says to the girl:

"Go you and get one o' them there pies. I dare say they've come again by now."

The girl went to the larder and she looked, but, of course, there wasn't anything on the shelf except the five dishes. Back she came to her mother.

"No, Mother! Them pies haven't come again!"

"Not one of 'em?" says the mother.

"Not one of 'em," says the girl.

"Well, come again, or not come again," says the woman, "I'll have one for supper."

"But you can't, Mother! Not if they haven't come again!" says the girl.

"But I can," says her Mother. "Go and bring the best of 'em."

"Best or worst," says the girl, "I've been and ate them all."

Well, the woman was so flabbergasted at what her daughter had told her that she didn't answer a word. She just took her spinning wheel to the front door and began to work. As she span, she sang:

"My daughter have ate five, five pies today!
My daughter have ate five, five pies today!"

Now, just then the King came riding down the street and he heard her singing, but what the words might be he couldn't hear, so he stopped and he said:

"What are you a-singing, my good woman?"

Now she felt ashamed to let the King know what a greedy girl her daughter had been, so she sang him different words:

"My daughter have spun five, five skeins today.
My daughter have spun five, five skeins today."

"Stars o' mine!" said the King. "I never heard tell of any girl that could do that!" Then, sitting there on his horse, he thought for a bit and at last he said:

"I want a wife and I'll marry your daughter. But mind," says he, "there'll be a bargain! Eleven months out of the year she shall have all the vittles she likes to eat and all the gowns she likes to wear and all the company she likes to keep; but in the last month of the year she'll have to

186

spin five skeins every day. If she doesn't, it'll be off with her head."

The woman thought a bit.

"Done!" says she at last. The girl gave her word as well, for, of course, they both thought what a grand marriage that would be. As for spinning five skeins every day, why, when the time came, there'd surely be plenty of ways of getting out of that.

"Likeliest by then the King'll have forgotten all about it," thinks the mother.

So they were married. Sure enough, for eleven months everything went well. The girl had all the vittles she liked to eat and all the gowns she liked to wear and all the company she liked to keep.

But when the eleven months were nearly up, she began to think about those five skeins now and again and to wonder if the King still had them in mind. However, he didn't say a word about them and, of course, neither did she.

"Likeliest he's forgot all about 'em," thinks the girl.

However, the evening of the last day came and what do you think the King did? He took her to a room in the castle that she'd never set eyes on before. There wasn't anything in it except a spinning wheel, a stool, and a little narrow bed. Then the King said:

"Here you are, my dear! You'll be shut up in this room tomorrow with some vittles and some flax and if you haven't spun five skeins by the night, your head'll have to come off!" And with that, away he went about his business.

Well, the girl was fairly frightened out of her life! Your see she'd always been such a careless, idle girl that she didn't know how to spin at all – let alone how to spin five skeins all in one day. So now what was she going to do next day, when she was to be shut up in that room with no one to come nigh nor near to help her? She sat down on a stool in the kitchen, and lor! how she did cry!

All of a sudden she heard a sort of knocking – low down on the kitchen door it was. She upped and she opened the door and what should she see outside but a little black thing. Like a little old man it was, only that it had a long tail. That queer little thing looked up at her out of its squint eyes and said:

"What are you a-crying for?"

"What's that to you?" says the girl.

"Never you mind," it said. "Just you tell me what you're a-crying for."

"'Twouldn't do no good if I did tell you," says she.

"How do you know it wouldn't?" it said. As it spoke, it twirled its long tail.

"Well," says the girl, "I suppose 'twouldn't do no harm to tell even if it didn't do any good."

So with that, she told the little black thing the whole tale, first and last – all about the pies and the skeins and the King, what she and her mother had thought, and what the King had said and the horrid empty room and everything.

When she'd done telling, the

little thing thought for a while and then it said:

"This is what I'll do. I'll come to the window of that room every morning and I'll take away the flax and I'll bring it back, all spun, every night."

Well, now it was the girl's turn to think. "What's your pay?" says she.

That little black thing looked out of the corners of its squinty eyes and said:

"Pay? Oh, nothing much! I'll just give you three guesses every night to find out my name. Then, if you haven't guessed it afore the month's up, you'll be mine!"

"Done!" says she – you see, she felt sure she'd be able to guess its name.

"All right!" says that black imp, and lor! how it twirled its tail! There wasn't another word between them and before she could think, the little thing was gone.

Next day, sure enough, the King took her into the empty room that he'd shown her before. There was nothing in it except the spinning wheel, the flax, the stool, the narrow bed and the day's vittles.

"There you are!" says the King. "And if that flax isn't spun up this night, off goes your head!" With that he went out and locked the door behind him.

He'd hardly gone, when what should the girl hear but a knocking. It wasn't at the door this time, it was low down on the window.

She upped and opened it and there was that little black thing standing on the window ledge.

"Where's that flax?" it says in its sharp little voice.

"Here it is," says she and she handed it out.

Well, there the girl sat and did nothing all day except eat up the vittles. Come evening, the knocking came again at the window. The girl upped and she opened it. There was that little black thing and sure enough it had five skeins of beautiful spun flax over its arm.

"Here's the work! Now what's my name?" it says.

"Is it BILL?" says she.

"No, it isn't," it says and it twirled its tail.

"Is it NED?" says she.

"No, it isn't," it says and it twirled its tail harder.

"Is it MARK?" says she.

"No, it isn't!" it says and it grinned and twirled its tail still faster and flew away out of the window.

When the King came in, a bit later, there were the five skeins well spun and all ready for him.

"I see I shan't have to have your head off tonight, my dear," says he. "You'll have your vittles and your

flax in the morning as before." With that away he goes.

Well, so it went on. Every day the flax and the vittles were brought
to the girl and every day the little black imp used to come in, mornings
and evenings. All day the girl would sit trying to think of names to
say when it came at night. But, try as she would, she never seemed
to hit on the right one.

As it got on toward the end of the month, the imp began to look very
maliceful and pleased with itself and twirled its tail faster and faster.

At last it came to the last day except one. That imp came at night, as
usual, with the five skeins. It grinned and said:

"What, my dear, haven't you got my name yet?"

"Is it NICODEMUS?" says she.

"No, 'tisn't," it says.

"Is it SAMUEL?" says she.

"No, 'tisn't," it says.

"Ah, well, is it METHUSELAH?" says she.

"No, 'tisn't that neither," it says.

Then it looks at her with eyes like coals of fire
and says:

"Woman! There's only tomorrow night left AND
THEN YOU'LL BE MINE!" And away it flew.

As you can guess, the girl felt really horrid!
However, it wasn't long before she heard the King
coming along the passage. In he came and when he
saw the five skeins he said to her:

"Well, my dear, I don't see but what you'll have
your skeins ready tomorrow as well, just like the other
nights. I reckon I shan't have your head cut off, so I'll
have supper in here with you tonight."

So supper was brought in for the two of them and
another stool for the King and down they sat.

Now the King hadn't eaten but a mouthful or so,
when he stops and begins to laugh.

"What is it?" says she.

"Ah, why," says he, "I was out hunting today and I came to a place in the wood I'd never seen before. There was an old chalk pit among the trees. It seemed to me that I could hear a sort of humming. I got off my horse and I crept right quiet to the edge of that chalk pit and I looked down. What should I see but the funniest little black thing you ever set eyes on. What that thing was a-doing you'll never guess! It had a little spinning wheel and it was a-spinning wonderful fast. As it spun it kept on twirling its tail and singing."

"What did it sing?" asked the girl softly, trying to keep very quiet.

"The funniest words!" said the King. "Over and over it sang them like this:

Ninny ninny not,
My name's Tom-Tit-Tot."

When the girl heard this, she could
have jumped out of her skin with
joy, but she didn't say a word about it to the King, no,
not though they talked friendly-like all the rest of the
evening.

Next morning, when it came for the flax, that little
black thing looked more maliceful than ever! In the evening, that imp
knocked hard at the windowpane, ever so much bolder!

The girl opened the window and this time that thing didn't stay out
on the ledge, but came right in, right down on to the floor of the room.
It was grinning from ear to ear and its tail was twirling round so fast!

"What's my name?" it says, as it gave her the skeins.

"Is it SOLOMON?" says she, pretending to be frightened.

"No, 'tisn't!" it says, and that imp came a bit nearer to her.

"Well, is it ZEBEDEE?" says she again.

"No, 'tisn't!" says the imp, and that little black thing laughed and
twirled its tail till you couldn't hardly see it!

"Take time, woman!" it says. "Take time. Remember – NEXT
GUESS AND YOU'RE MINE!" It stretched out its horrid black hands at her.

But with that the girl stepped back a pace or two. She looked that
black imp in the eye and she laughed out loud. She pointed her finger at
it and she called out:

"Ninny ninny not,
Your name's Tom-Tit-Tot!"

When it heard her say the words, it shrieked most
horribly. But a bargain's a bargain, so away it had to
fly into the dark and she never saw it again.

This is a Suffolk version of a widely known
nursery classic. The Brothers Grimm recorded
what is virtually the same tale in their
Rumpelstiltskin. Habetrot and Scatlie
Mab *and* Whuppity Stourie *are Yorkshire
and Scottish versions but with a slightly
different moral.*

*All the tales are based on the widespread
belief that to know the name of a hostile person,
or thing, gives power.*